Troika To Utopia
Part 2

4.11.13

Troika To Utopia
Part 2

A Docu-drama in Three-Quarter Time

Louis A. Coppola

authorHOUSE®

AuthorHouse™
1663 Liberty Drive
Bloomington, IN 47403
www.authorhouse.com
Phone: 1-800-839-8640

Published by AuthorHouse 08/29/2012

ISBN: 978-1-4772-0577-8 (sc)
ISBN: 978-1-4772-0578-5 (e)

Also by

Louis A. Coppola:

Essay-fiction Books

Homecrest Avenue, Silhouettes of an Accidental Family

C.B.S, The Chucklehead Broadcasting System

Plays

Chiaroscuro

Troika To Utopia, Part One

Troika To Utopia, Part Two (A Docu-drama In Three-Quarter Time)

Television

Checkmate, ABC/TV, The Benson Series

You can fool some of the people all of the time,
And all of the people some of the time, but you
Can't fool all of the people all the time.

Abraham Lincoln

♥

CHARACTERS PART TWO

(Some double as other characters)
Coachie,—50's; guide; quasi repentant liar; double as other characters; wears blue or red suit and yellow shoes.
Mamushka—ageless; Mother Russia, can double as Stalin's wife and others
Kerensky, 40's, Prime Minister of Provisional Government before coup; wears puttees.
An Aide-di-camp, 30's.
Chiedze, 40's; party official.
Kollantai, Marie—30's; Bolshevik party official; free love advocate.
Bouch-Bruevich, 30's; PR head of Bolshevik propaganda.
Lenin, 50's; d, 1924; leader of Bolshevik Party.
Nadya Krupskaya, 40's; his wife; confident and amanuensis.
Inessa Armand, 40's; Lenin's lover and party amanuensis.
Trotsky, 50's; heir apparent to Lenin.
Zinoviev, Grigorii Eseyevich, 40's; close Lenin associate.
Kransky, 40's; radical lawyer with Provisional Government.
Stalin, 50's; d, 1953; dictator 1927–1953; ambitious; devoid of conscience.
Beria, Lavrenti Pavlovich–Stalin hit man after 1938; NKVD chairman 1941–43;
Svetlana, 20's; Stalin's daughter.
Nadezhda "Nadya" Sergeyevna Alliluyeva, 20's, her mother and Stalin's wife.
Bukharin, 50's; d, 1936 or 38; member of Lenin's Old Guard.
Shotman, 40's; a Bolshevik.
Sukhanov, 40's; disappeared around 1930; journalist; and Bolshevik.
Galena, 30's; his wife
Uritsky, 40's; a Bolshevik.
Zverdlov, 40's; a loyal Bolshevik.
Martov–a Menshevik; split from Lenin around 1904.
Bogdanov, 40's; a Menshevik.
Lunacharsky, 40's; a Menshevik.
Fanya or Doris "Fanny" Kaplan, 20's; radical socialist revolutionary; shot Lenin 1918.
Maxim Gorky, 40's; novelist–playwright; socialist.
Tsar Nicholas (Nicky) Romanov, 40's; d, 1918.
Tsarina Alexandra (Sonny), his wife; 30's; d, 1918.
Rasputin, 30's; d, December 1917; lewd, dissolute monk with unusual powers
Prince Felix Yusupov, 30 a nobleman conspirator–killer of Rasputin.
Baker, 50's.
The Rabble—various citizens, workers, peasants, police, Cossacks, and military.

MUSIC: Waltz, i.e., The Emperor's waltz; Jazz Suite No 1, Shostakovich.

STYLE: Limbo and thrust; characters exchange dialogue but also address the audience in a docu-drama series of monologues and dramatic interplay. Possible: dance sequence on ice skates.

PART TWO

Preamble: The Case Placed Before Mamushka.

Mamushka: Who are you?
Lenin: Lenin. I died in 1924.
Mamushka: Congratulations. What are you doing here?
Lenin: Somebody called me.
Mamushka: Not me.
Kerensky: I did. Look. To make a long story short–
Lenin: That'll be a first.
Kerensky: Defeatist!
Lenin: Bourgeois compromiser.
Mamushka: Silence! Sit. Before I put you over my knee. Now, Coachie—where are you? Ah, there you are. Slava bohu! Put down that bottle. It's not mother's milk. You were saying. (Louder.) You were saying. Nekita Sergeivnov!!
Coachie: Yes. I was, saying—(Coughs.) What? O, yes. No. Wasn't that. (Suggests female.) Where are my notes? (Sees bottle in hand.) O, there you are, old pal! (Points at bottle.) So, you were saying?
Mamushka: (At bread line.) The revo–lution.
Coachie: Oo . . . that. (Crosses self.) Slava bohu! St Petersburg, Russia, March 1917: Long breadlines, mothers standing in freezing weather, day and night for weeks and months, warming themselves by ash can fires, (Lights up on bread queue.) their children with bellies swollen from hunger, cadavers—Yes. Ca–davers (Gets maudlin.) sil–houetted against this ghostly gravestone city while traitors and German saboteurs slink about disrupting the economy, subverting the war effort, and at any moment the threat of German Zeppelins. *When government fails in its duty it is the people's right to rebel!*

ACT 1,

Scene 1

Time: March, 1917; early, chaotic days of the first revolution
Place: Petersburg, Russia Bread queue to a bakery; an ash can fire.)

Baker: Quota filled for today. Come back tomorrow.
Mamushka: Tomorrow my baby will be dead.
Baker: Then you'll have one less mouth to feed. (Slams door; SHE throws a rock through the bakery window; other mothers follow suit.)
Crowd: Bread! Give us Bread! (Men from factories join the melee.)
Coachie: When police and soldiers arrive they wisely decide against shooting women and children, join in, and rioting spreads turning stone into fire. (Mother resumes part of Mamushka, sits and observes with watchful eye. A citizen enters, exits chased by Workers; explosions, gunfire.) St Petersburg, city of stone, Peter the Great's Russo–Venetian window on the West designed by Italian architects, built by the sweat and blood of countless Russians who were maimed or died of hunger and exposure in the crush of metal and stone that went into its senseless construction. Petrograd speaks for those nameless workers who left a city rising out of the cold northern waters like a bleak mausoleum, one of those fairytale kingdoms that you love because you never question it. But walk around Pete, drink it up with your gut. In winter temperatures drop to minus 30 c. The wind off the Nevsky is razor sharp. The only daylight is from 10 AM to 3 PM, and nights are an eerie chalky white, then you will question the point of it, and conclude, it is the dream of a madman. But then what is life but madness? Tfu! Nasdrovia!
Citizen 1: (Returns in audience.) Sir, Madame, I beg you, please. Let me in.

Workers 1 and 2: You there! Halt! Your palms. No calluses. Like a baby's ass.
Citizen 1: My index finger. Look.
Worker 1 and 2: Bourgeois pencil pusher. Run on the count of three. (He runs off.) One, two, three! (Shoots gun in the air.) Ha, ha. You there. What's your business? Where to, Citizen? Hands. Palms up.
Worker 2: Look at them ham hocks. What's in the bag, Chubby Fingers?
Coachie: A caliper and Tri–square.
Worker 2: Oh, a dentist.
Worker 1: And your father?
Coachie: A miner and pipe metal fitter.
Worker 1: Go in peace. (Coachie steps back.) Say, comrade, have you heard? There's a revolution.
Worker 2: No! Where?
Worker 1: Beats me. I'm a tourist myself.
Worker 2: Aren't we all! (Citizens run in and out; enter Kerensky.)
Coachie: Triumphant and jubilant, people were unaware of the miracle they had achieved—the toppling of three hundred years of Romanovs.
Kerensky: Hope had still to catch up with reality.
Coachie: Alexander Kerensky ex–Prime Minister of the Provisional Government.
Kerensky: The unimaginable had yet to sink in. People vacillated between the emotions of a conquering hero–
Coachie: And going on tiptoe expecting sudden counter attacks round every corner and bend. Tfu! (Sneaks a drink.)
Kerensky: Joy mixed with fear in a mood that was at once elated and suspicious in a bittersweet time. In April 1917 the revolution was young and wild, indiscreet, and without direction.
Coachie: Individuals and groups clashed with one another, and if you had nothing to do: that smelled of the aristocracy, and something was found for you to do like hanging at the end of a rope. Tfu!
Kerensky: People gathered by the thousands at Finland Station in a mix of peasants, workers, and soldiers in trucks and tanks,

Coachie: Then a strange monster appeared, the searchlight, big and blinding.
Kerensky: But a greater monster with a one–word name and no patronymic was about to descend on the unsuspecting people.

Scene 2
(Looters burst in on an aristocrat at dinner.)

Aristocrat: Moment, s'il vous plait. (They stop; he drinks, daubs lips, inclines his head:) Merci, mez ami. (Jumps out the window.)
Worker 2: There's a man knows how to die.
Worker 1: Bonehead. This is the first floor.
Worker 2: (Picks up plate.) What's this stinkin' stuff?
Worker 1: Poi–son, comrade.
Worker 2: Smells fishy.
Worker 1: You're the fishy one. Fish on a silver plate is poi–son.
Worker 2: (Dumps food; uses plate as a mirror.) I think I need a shave.
Worker 1: You need a new face. (Grabs plate shoves it in his coat.)
Worker 2: Here cockroaches eat better than us.
Worker 1: That was then. This is now, a new day.
Worker 2: I'll believe it this time next month. (Several men burst in wearing stolen attire; one wears an over sized fur coat with driving goggles.)
Worker 3: There's a meeting at Finland Station. We go.
Worker 2: In that coat we'll be mistaken for nobles and shot.
Worker 1: You they'll give a mop and a bucket.
Worker 3: Somebody important.
Worker 2: Who?
Worker 1: Your mother. You been a naughty boy! Ain't said your prayers.
Worker 3: Somebody named Lenin.
Worker 1: More bourgeois monkey business. Here's your *linen*. (Yank tablecloth tosses it at him.)

Worker 3: My farmhouse can fit in this room. (At sidebar.) What's this thing?
Worker 1: A fingerbowl.
Worker 3: I don't see no fingers.
Worker 1: Here's five in your face.
Worker 2: (Examining an antique chair.) Whose ass is this skinny?
Worker 1: Yours. You're half–assed. It's an–teek, com–rade.
Worker 2: (Looking underneath seat.) Khon–o, 1812. (Sits in chair and it breaks.) They don't make 'em like they used to.
Worker 1: True. After you they busted the mold. Let's get to the station.
Worker 3: (Tinkles servant bell.) Bring me my toilet paper. (Tosses bell.)
Worker 1: I haven't crapped in a week. Who's in charge? To hell with 'em.
Worker 3: Yeah. It's our revolution. I bake. I'll run the granary.
Worker 4: I oil train wheels.
Worker 1: You Head Transportation.
Worker 5: I got a telephone.
Worker 1: You run the phone Company. Anybody got a radio?
Worker 6: Me. I mean I do now. Hey, I found it.
Worker 1: Can you turn it on and off?
Worker 6: Yeah. Think I'm stupid?
Worker 1: Stupid enough. You're Head of Communication. Who has electricity?
Worker 7: I got candles.
Worker 1: Close enough. You Head Utilities.
Worker 8: I once stole a ruble from a blind man.
Worker 1: You run the banks.
Kerensky: The greatest revolution the world has ever seen was born without fanfare, or slogans from ideologists, but from hungry bellies, the elemental instinct for survival. There were no romantic connections underground or above to clandestine socialist gangs of one stripe or another, or to that damnable troika of Bull–shevik baloney artists.
Mamushka: Hold the mustard. What is a Bolshevik?
Martov: In 1903–

Mamushka: Don't talk history when the present eludes you.
Martov: Lenin proposed an amendment to our revolutionary constitution that was considered hard line Blanquist, a doctrine of the Paris Commune, i.e., direct action for the majority led by an active and highly organized minority.
Mamushka: Slava bohu! (God.) Somebody translate that.
Martov: Around the 1870's some Frenchies barricaded themselves in a section of Paris and proclaimed self–rule. Marx and Lenin admired them.
Mamushka: Two peas in a pod. Phew! What is that stink? (Waves hand to clear air. Stalin is up R back of a scrim smoking a pipe.) Go on. Speak plain.
Lenin: The Paris Commune was the prototype proletarian society. (Cheers.)
Martov: After Lenin's proposal was voted down many members went home. But Lenin kept hammering away, demanded another vote, and this time he won based on a minimum quorum. It split the party. From then on Lenin's group was snidely referred to as "bolshevki", or majority, and we were the "mensheviki", or minority. We "Mensheviks" saw ourselves as a loose organization striving to embrace the working class—(Lenin: Bah!) and the Socialist intelligentsia. We'd identify with them both.
Lenin: The working class is heterogeneous divided by differences of outlook, origin, sectional disparities. You'd embrace an octopus. Not all of the proletariat can achieve a high level of enlightenment. A few are steeped in superstition and ignorance, and cults like *the Silver Dove*. To grasp the whole is to be become heterogeneous, too, enjoining its weakness and strengths, its ignorance and socialist yearning, its backwardness, and its aspirations. We'd become a stodgy representation of the working class instead of its inspirer, leader and organizer. The natural urge of the workers toward socialism would lead to trade unionism, which is in bed with capitalism. We cannot depend on the inborn socialism of the people. The party must consist of a selected body embracing only the most enlightened and courageous sections of the working class, its real vanguard, which would not be shy of determined and disciplined action.
Martov: That's Blanquism.

Lenin: No. I reject the idea that the only method of revolution is direct action by a conspiratorial minority ignoring the will of the majority. Revolution wins if wanted, but the majority has to be led by an active, highly organized minority.

Kerensky: We'll correct that bit of poetry soon enough.

Coachie: In 1902 we were condemned to starvation by a bankrupt autocracy. In 1904 we fought a war with Japan and lost. In villages hunger was the normal condition. Then came Bloody Sunday, a peaceful march in Nevsky Square for an audience with the Tsar was greeted by bullets. The question was how much longer would this bankrupt autocrat live from day to day by patching holes in his political and financial budget with skin from the living body of the people?

Kerensky: The workers began to vent their feelings crying Nicholas, the Deceiver! Nicholas, the Bloody, the Hangman! It was Easter Monday, no newspapers were on sale, shops were closed and the troops off duty. Thousands of workers, peasants, soldiers, and bureaucrats converged in the Finland Square Train Station—a pivotal East–West stop on the Baltic for departures and arrivals between Pete and Finland. Moving was impossible: troops with bands, red and gold arches in the station, red flags, outlines of armored cars stood above the crowd. The greeting platform was decorated in red and gold banners with inscriptions: Lenin Arrives! Meet Lenin!" The Bolsheviks bally–hood the people to welcome Lenin the "illustrious revolutionary" and "émigré". But there was more to it than met the eye. Much of it was a distraction to cover–up the bigger question, how did Lenin get through enemy territory? (Lights up L.)

Coachie: On the Welcome Platform is Marie Alexandra Kollantai, free love advocate, and future Party diplomat. The cheerful, broad shouldered man is Vladimir Bouch–Bruevich in charge of party literature, greetings and arrangements and the others are entourage.

Bouch–Bruevitch: Move right. Left. Back up a tad. I adore you.

Kollantai: (Checking her notes.) Comrade, Lenin, on behalf of—O, God! I can't.

Bouch–Bruevitch: The lady with lace kerchief on her head, speaks in prose, walks in poetry.

Kollantai: Cut the nonsense. I'm nervous enough. Where do I stand?
Bouch–Bruevitch: At the heart of my world.
Kollantai: Good God! Are you after something?
Bouch–Bruevitch: A kiss, a hug, a look.
Kollantai: You're an animal. Behave. Speeches make me nervous.
Bouch–Bruevitch: Be brief. Before you know it fini. How about this, comrade (Pinches her rear.), to bring you down to earth?
Kollantai: Comrade, you're so suave. Hold these flowers. (HE complies, she goes back of him, knees him in the butt.) That's for not showing up last night. (Smiling he waves to people; she takes flowers.) Thank you, comrade.
Bouch–Bruevitch: No. Thank you, comrade. I love aggression. May I return the compliment?
Kollantai: I'll be home waiting.
Bouch–Bruevitch: Splendid. (Arranging décor.) O, the lady with lace on her head talks in poetry, but walks in prose. Move left, no right.
Kollantai: Left, right, which?
Bouch–Bruevitch: Right where you are.
Kollantai: You're sure?
Bouch–Bruevitch: Yes. No. Well, yes. Good. Your speech ready?
Kollantai: Yes. But I'm not. I may throw up.
Bouch–Bruevitch: Then smile, turn away, do it in the bouquet and continue.
Kollantai: I'm higher than a kite. Pinch me and I'll wake up. (HE complies.) Again. I guess I'm not dreaming. Again, comrade. Oo.
Bouch–Bruevitch: I'm going to peel you like an onion. Stand over here. Just kidding. You're fine there.
Kollantai: We prayed for this day. Suddenly I feel like crying.
Bouch–Bruevitch: O, the lady with lace kerchief speaks in prose, but walks in poetry. I adore you, kiss your cheeks. Incidentally, Lenin hates flowers. Give them to Chiedze to give to Lenin. They hate each other anyway. (Spot on.)
Coachie: Lenin arrived in March–
Chiedze: April.
Coachie: March by the Orthodox Russian–
Chiedze: No. The Gregorian, or was it the Julian?

Inessa: The old calendar is from Caesar and the Romans. The Gregorian is from St. Gregory, the middle ages. Before Lenin it was Julian after him Gregorian.
Nadya: One is ahead and the other behind by nine days.
Bogdanov: I'll tell my landlord when the rent is due.
Lunacharsky: Go ahead and sleep in the park with me.
Sukhanov: There was a chill in the air. A mist.
Chiedze: It was warm. No. Brisk. The moon was low.
Lunacharsky: In Nevsky Square–
Nadya: Catherine Hall.
Coachie: Trotsky was with him.
Nadya: He was in the Bronx.
Trotsky: Nova Scotia and then England. I was detained in both places.
Coachie: Stalin was with Lenin.
Zinoviev: No. He was in Siberia.
Mamushka: Maybe nobody arrived and you're all dreaming.
Lunacharsky: Lenin jumped from the train.
Chiedze: Stepped.
Coachie: He casually walked on–
Chiedze: Ran on. Lenin ran on and then he was casual. I know. I was there. I introduced him. The man ran on carrying flowers, wearing a bowler and black overcoat. Do you understand? "Ran," as in "to run," and then he was casual.
Coachie: Casual.
Chiedze: Yes, casual, as in nonchalant.
Coachie: Nonchalant.
Chiedze: He was seemingly unaware of what was happening. I called for silence. When the noise died down I go, *on behalf of the Petrograd Committee with the cooperation of the military organization.* There were hoots and howls. Finally, a hush came over the crowd. Someone coughed, a baby cried, and I thought Lenin's carrying a bouquet of flowers bigger than he is. How incongruous. I nearly laughed out loud. Why flowers? This was no school prom. Flowers in March? I couldn't get my mind off the flowers. Lenin hated flowers. Oriental almond eyes, the devil's own, peering out from among the flowers that must've come straight from Crimea

where jagged mountains rise from the blue emerald waters with acacia, apple, peach, cherry, lilacs, and violets.

Coachie: Lenin's suit was gray.

Nadya: Black.

Inessa: Crumpled and baggy.

Coachie: He wore the worker's peek cap.

Nadya: A bowler.

Inessa: The cap he became famous for came later.

Kerensky: So what did he say, comrade?

Chiedze: That crumpled suit, frayed at the edges, baggy at the knees, soon became a knight's armor, I can tell you. At first the crowd didn't know what to make of him. To most he never existed. Here was this virulent, hungry crowd champing at the bit and Lenin standing there holding a bouquet of flowers.

Coachie: Wait. Lenin came on carrying flowers. You were already out there. Did you run off and come back with flowers?

Chiedze: No. I came back and then ran off.

Coachie: Who gave you the flowers?

Chiedze: Probably a Menshevik who knew Lenin hated flowers. I introduced Lenin. *Comrades,* I go. Wait. First, I must tell you why Lenin hated flowers.

Mamushka: Just tell us what he said.

Chiedze: I go, *Comrade Lenin,* and he sneezes, a–chew! *In the name of the Petrograd Soviet—*A–chew!*—And the whole revolution, welcome to Russia.* I could eat those words now. *We consider the chief task of the revolutionary democracy at present is to defend our revolution.* Someone yells, (Fay.) "With Flowers?" The crowd laughed while tragedy hovered in the wings.

Nadya: (Stepping Dwn C.) It was early morning and Ilych wanted to walk to our quarters on Shiroskaya Street to take in the city, the air, and buildings. On the way Ilych addressed various crowds.

Inessa: Extemporaneously, from the bonnet of several cars.

Bogdanov: And the flowers?

Nadya: Tossed into a canal.

Lunacharsky: The heels of his shoes were worn out.

Nadya: No. Volodya disliked worn heels and always bought a new pair.

Chiedze: Wait. I remember now. First I signaled Kollantai to start her introductory speech. She comes forward, a pale face, beads of sweat on her forehead, hands Lenin the flowers and goes back. Someone yelled, get on with it, comrade! So I step up to fill the gap. Frankly, nobody knew what to make of Lenin. To most people he was unknown, a shabby figure in a frayed baggy suit. To me he was rather elfin, yes, elfin with red hair on a high forehead, a goatee and those almond eyes, a character out of Grimm, or more precisely Puck out of A Mid–Summer Night's Dream. (Mimicking.) *The chief task of the revolution is to defend it against every kind of attack from within and without.* He pauses, looks around calmly examining the ceiling of the Tsar's Room–

Nadya: What ceiling? It was outside.

Zinoviev: It was in Catherine Hall.

Nadya: That was the next night.

Inessa: The hall was mobbed, overflowing with peasants and workers–

Nadya: Craning their necks to see, to hear.

Inessa: Soldiers carrying weapons stood on stools and chairs–

Nadya: Dirty booted illiterates belonging to no special political persuasion.

Lunacharsky: We shouted to be heard in normal conversation.

Kerensky: Comrade Chiedze, you were saying *the chief task of the revolution–*

Chiedze: Not me. Lenin.

Kerensky: *Is to defend it.* Against what?

Nadya: The West, the bourgeoisie, the aristocracy, counter–revolution.

Chiedze: I go, *Comrade Lenin, we invite you*—No. *We hope that you will join us in striving toward this goal.* Meanwhile, Lenin is looking about indifferently. I could've choked him. He looks over the crowd, and starts re–arranging that stupid bouquet of flowers.

Kerensky: What were his words, comrade?

Chiedze: His body language said it all. Standing apart, looking off, he even dares to turn completely away from the delegates of the Executive Committee. What nerve, I thought. Most of the crowd didn't know Lenin, or the meaning of émigré, let alone spell it. They hadn't read his works because they couldn't read or write. Then, too, Lenin had been living in exile two decades and this crowd was a new generation. Slowly he offset the hunger in their bellies and fear in their hearts. They weren't used to having the authorities on their side. They'd busted three hundred years of servitude, a fantastic and unimaginable thing. Their thoughts seesawed between dreamy exhilaration and expectation of sudden reprimand and reprisal from those they'd ousted.

Kerensky: You've got me seesawing. Get on with it.

Chiedze: He goes, (Exaggerated fay voice.) *Dear comrades, dear workers, dear sailors, and dear soldiers.* I wanted to stick those flowers up his dear anal aperture. *During the journey here I was expecting to be taken straight from the station to Peter and Paul.* Russia should've been so lucky. He should've been locked up. The key tossed in the Neva. The murderous son–of–a–bitch! *But no,* he says, *we are far from that, it seems.* (Cheers.) *I'm happy to greet you in the name of the victorious Russian revolution, you, the advanced guard of the international proletarian army.* My God! We were still trying to figure out what was around the next corner and he mentions an *international proletarian army*. I thought, what's all this worldwide crap? We were expecting bombs any minute from the Kaiser's zeppelins and he's talking about embracing Germans, and refers to German socialists nobody knows. Some said, he's crazy. Out of step with reality. *At the summons of our comrades Karl Liebknecht and Rosa Luxemburg the people will turn their weapons against their capitalist exploiters.* Right. Just like that. The man was seeing things. *The revolution achieved by you has now opened a new epoch . . . The hour is not far away when people everywhere will turn their weapons against their imperialist governments. You have been educated far too long by the Tsar's whip.* He was cheered and jeered. The man knew how to speak, believe me. He held his position. He had guts. In the end, his absurd political platform became Party Doctrine. There was nothing remarkable here, yet the crowd responded like wild animals. The change was amazing. Then what he'd done came to me. Simply, briefly, succinctly, Lenin touched the people's spirit, voiced everything they felt, and in an instant he embodied the revolution. The screams and applause were thunderous, infectious, and deafening. Even I applauded, sneezing and shouting. Lenin! Lenin! Who knows why? Lenin! Lenin! Lenin!

Nadya–Inessa: At dawn that first day we all walked to Shirokaya Street. The Party arranged for our quarters with Anna and Mark Timofeyetch. We passed through armed groups marching and singing. Singing and shouting. Criss crossing in absolute exhilaration.

Nadya: You wanted it to last forever. I took hold of Vovachka's arm.

Inessa: And I Vova's other arm. (Diminutives for Vladimir.)

Nadya: Have you eyes to see, a heart to believe?

Lenin: This has really opened my eyes for the first time to the true meaning and role of an uprising. One cannot know the guts of it unless they're in it. The whole thing is infectious. The air bristles with new life, new possibilities.

Nadya and Inessa: Everywhere people shouted: Long lives the Revolution! I felt light as a bird. Power to the people! Lifted out of my shoes. At first it was too fantastic to believe. There is an esprit de corps. One for all, all for one. A sense of unity. No class division. Is this real, the dream realized?

Nadya: Anna and Mark had adopted a child, Gora.

Inessa: Sleeping peacefully in the arms of oblivion.

Nadya: While outside Humpty–Dumpty had fallen.

Inessa: All the King's horses and all the King's men embraced the revolution.

Nadya: O, how I wanted to hold that child in my arms, feel it against my breasts—(Lenin moves to daub her tears.) Don't. Stop. (Pulling away.) I hardly spoke to Ilych that first night.

Inessa: Words were impediments to the visceral joy better expressed by hosannas in a deaf and dumb dance.

Nadya: Ilych left a note on Gora's pillow, "Workers of the World Unite!" As he stepped out on the balcony to speak to the crowd gathered in front of the building I took off his bowler and handed him a worker's cap.

Lenin: (Motioning for silence.) Dear comrades, workers, sailors, and soldiers, I greet you in the name of *the victorious Russian revolution*, you, the *advanced guard of the international proletarian army.* (Cheers.) At the summons of our German comrades Liebnecht and Luxemburg the people of Germany will soon turn on their capitalist exploiters. The hour is fast approaching when people *everywhere* will turn against their imperialist oppressors. (Cheers.) In 1872 the narods (dark masses), peasants and populists, threw the 1st bomb under the Tsar's carriage while crossing Catherine Canal in Petersburg, killing horses and injuring the military escort. As the Tsar stepped from his carriage to tend the wounded, a second fatal bomb landed at his feet. Horrible? Yes.

Crowd Voice: Live by the sword, die by the sword. (Cheering.)

Lenin: How often have those imperial carriages run you down . . . and your children . . . and never looked back? Early on the Narodnaya Volya, our dark people, accepted *terrorism* as self–defense; others thought it too aggressive, still others saw it as strategic assassination of high officials designed to panic and force concessions. But isolated acts of terror do not work. No sooner does one tyrant go down then another springs up worse than his predecessor. (Hoots and howls.) In 1905 the people led by Father Gapon in a peaceful protest to petition the tsar were gunned down by his imperialist guard—(Boo!) The people tucked tail and did not retaliate. Why? Because they still believed in the "Little Father" Tsar Nicholas Romanov,—(Booing.) and because their anger had not reached the tipping point of endurance. As a result of all this we've come down to three years of a rotten imperialist war with no end in sight. And, let's not forget, the filthy, manipulative bourgeoisie was well organized . . . masters of class warfare. The people were not sufficiently class conscious to recognize their misery was no accident, but by design. The rich live by usury and exploitation caressing you with one hand choking you with the other. Change takes what you have done—a concerted, undaunted effort by the people . . . forceful and determined . . . dedicated to freedom and resolved to fight until the will of the people prevails. (Cheers.) I need not tell you what is in your hearts, but I say it to the doubters: Bread, comrades, means more than democracy. Every day brings new horrors from the war. Your children, not those of the aristocracy or the bourgeoisie, return from the front demoralized, maimed and dead . . . *and some their parents will never see again because they were blown to smithereens by German canons, and pieces of what was once a living human* *being lie strewn about on some distant battlefield of no strategic value.* To them I say, *Where is your benevolent Little Father or God in this carnage?* Everyday men are dying by the thousands on all sides while at home the people "trustingly ignorant" still believe in their ministers. Even here now some among us believe in the temporary government. Those same professed comrades were brain washed by the whip of imperialism, and the degenerate dog–eat–dog capitalist mentality. To them I say if that's your position we must part ways. I prefer to be in a minority. To them I cry *mockery!* To them I say what do you know of the secret agreements behind closed doors between allies that carve up countries and lives like butchers in a knackery? You know nothing! To them I say your trust has been misplaced . . . Take back that trust . . . Invest it in yourself. Demand peace without annexations. The people of countries Russia is fighting are your brothers and sisters . . . like you they have <u>no say in anything</u>. Time to end *Pinocchio Politics!* Those noses keep getting longer. To our contemptible leaders it boils down to the poor cleaning up the dirty work of the rich. *This . . . must . . . be . . . clearly understood! Our revolution must bring about a Soviet Republic, a liberated society,* a state run by the workers for the workers, a dictatorship of the proletariat! On on your backs is a war you didn't ask for, the strongest example of betrayal of your trust in leaders to do right by you. I speak not only of a rotten imperialist war, but secret deals with so–called allies. (Crowd: What deals?) Russia gets Constantinople, the Dardanelles, and Mesopotamia as the spoils of victory. Let us be clear. *Our revolution must bring about a Soviet Republic for which the Paris Commune serves as a prototype, a community of workers run by workers.* Make no mistake. You have done a miraculous thing, you the advanced guard of the proletarian revolution. Pat each other on the back. Frankly, I had begun to doubt this day would come in my lifetime. (Voices: But there you are, comrade!) Yes. Here I am, and there you are, and we're not dead yet! I have only three words for you: Peace! Land! And Bread! (Voice: "That's four, comrade!" Laughter.) See there? In the *new* Russia we must contend with people who know their A, B, C's! (Cheers.) Enjoy your glorious triumph. Bask in it. You deserve it. (Cheers.) You are rewriting history. But the battle is not over. Do not lose sight of what still needs to be done. (Voice: What's that?) Securing your gains. Tonight when you are sleeping, even now at this moment, those you've ousted are not sleeping, but burning the midnight oil scheming of ways to regain what you have rightfully taken. In fact, they've already wormed their way back and some are already in place. (Crowd Voice: Who? Where?) The bourgeois foot of the Temporary Government is already in the door, their greedy paws reaching into your pocket. Keep vigil! Mark it. Tonight we say to the world of whore mongering capitalists, imperialist–autocrats, to a decadent "Pinocchio" Bourgeoisie, and shameless corporate elite, to them we say, *The battle has just begun! Business as usual is over! Oblige us with your absence. Peace! Land! Bread! Free–dom!* (Lights fade to cheers and singing of The International.)

ACT 2

A Post Mortem of Accountability

Scene 1

Place: The Sidewalk tables of The Pearly Gates Bistro.
Time: Limbo. (Note: Tried in Absentia: A public trial of dead souls.)

Kerensky: There you have it, the nut in a nutshell. After years in exile, no sooner does Lenin, that émigré vagabondo, set foot in Russia then he proclaims an international proletarian army. He dreams, as his real name implies: Vladimir—conqueror of the world. We shall see, comrades. The people had no idea of what Lenin implied, but Lenin, the opportunist, he knew. Don't kid yourself.
Coachie: And if you're schizophrenic don't kid yourselves. Ha. Tfu!
Kerensky: It was his last bid for power. He would gamble today on an unknown tomorrow using people for collateral. *No imperialist war,* he cried. Yah! (German accent.) Labeled me, Kerensky, Prime Minister of the Provisional Government, a *defencist* and *bourgeois lackey,* but what was Heir Lenin, that Janus holier than thou monomaniac snake in the grass? Even before I was Prime Minister, I said, *Let us act democratically with benevolence toward the opposition.* I was no imperialist warmonger. The war was not my doing. But there it was in my lap. I wanted an honorable end, not with our tail between our legs. There is no respectful way to pull out of war. The powerful always know who threw in the towel and eventually come calling.
Aide: The Bolsheviks gave him a triumphal entry as a returning hero.

Kerensky: Clever of them to use the people's enthusiasm to hide the truth.
Aide: What truth? You mean the sealed train?
Kerensky: Yes. As soon as the crowd has cooled down the cat will be let out of the bag. Evidence is on its way from Germany: notes, letters, secret dispatches captured from a courier revealing Bolshevik–German collaboration. The front page of Pravda has been cleared and readied to expose the truth. Heir Lenin will have to answer to the Congress of Soviets for his *deal with the Kaiser* that let him travel unmolested by "private train" from Zurich through Germany. With this he has dropped the noose round his own neck, which the people will tighten. Meanwhile, use their street tactics, start rumors and innuendo: Bolshevik Traitors! Watch for Pravda exposé:

Penniless Émigrés Travel Free!
Unmolested Through Enemy Territory.
Beware, Petrograd, of An Infestation
Of The German Vermin Bolshevik Hermann.

Those Godless intellectual guttersnipes. They're dirty sheets and soiled pillows in an unmade bed full of lice, nasty bedbugs, and cockeyed dreams. Now, what about the Romanovs?
Aide: Ensconced in the palace as ordered.
Kerensky: Good. (To audience.) As head of the Provisional Government, I had the royal couple placed under house arrest for their safety. If the people in their rage had gotten hold of them something horroribile would've resulted. I had only met the royal couple once as part of a group attending some innocuous affair. Now as I was to discover on meeting them under totally different circumstances I got the distinct impression that the tsar was resigned to the situation, while the Tsarina retained the aloofness typical of her class that was slightly condescending. In my talks with the Tsar I found him direct, and open–minded. He gave me the *unspoken impression* that abdication had relieved him of a great burden. (Lights up on the Royal Couple.) As I say, this is my personal feeling and not from anything said. (To Romanovs.) I must set a basic ground rule. For now while here you will not

be allowed to sleep in the same room. In addition, when together during the day there will always be guards posted nearby. (Tsar nods acceptance; the Tsarina swallows it bitterly.) My reasoning is that I want independent answers to questions and feel it best to keep you apart.

Tsar: (Slightly relieved.) Yes, of course.

Kerensky: (To audience.) Either he had expected something worse, or he was glad to have a break from the Tsarina who impressed me as the more dominate of the two. I found her less forthcoming than the Tsar, and lacking the common sense he needed to make decisions. On the other hand, perhaps her presence was an embarrassing reminder that he had abdicated and failed in his duty. I must say that the Tsarina had little in common with the matron of imperial Rome who sacrificed her children for Rome. On the contrary, the Tsarina had sacrificed Russia for her son. (To Tsar.) There are some who speak freely of leadership as though it goes hand–in hand with escape clauses in the event of trouble. It is, has always been, a mistaken notion. There are consequences.

Tsar: I knew very well what it meant to rule. I had moments of great satisfaction, praise, honor, and adulation. But, if I may be candid, I always felt in the back of my head that I had an unending job; that my life was no different than an actor in a play who must continually rejuvenate his role, put on his face and never slacken before the people. Each day brought new problems on top of old ones. There were gains and losses, joy and humiliation. God forgive me, but it was altogether too much. And then my son, night and day, and my wife possessed by an *idée fixe*. She bore me four beautiful daughters–

Tsarina: I wanted desperately to give Nicky a male heir to the throne. Finally, I had a boy. O, how happy we were. A beautiful baby boy. The girls adored him. We all did, but then, I realized the boy was a bleeder. What could we do? What would you do?

Tsar: Dead leaves under the bed.

Tsarina: Let him bleed? Do you see?

Tsar: Nature has its way.

Tsarina: I was God fearing. Why me?

Tsar: Sonny became transfixed on the boy and acted in blind desperation.

Tsarina: I felt it was God's will–
Tsar: Cousins intermarrying. Nature abhors insularity.
Tsarina: If he fell the slightest bruise–
Tsar: His blood lacked coagulants.
Tsarina: He could bleed to death. Days were long to afternoon, afternoons long to night, nights long to morning every minute filled with a thousand frights.
Tsar: Who would've believed it?
Tsarina: Every time he ran or jumped my heart was in my throat. Only *our friend* could stop the bleeding.
Tsar: The devil incarnate. Who would've believed it? When I saw Rasputin for what he truly was–
Tsarina: What else could a mother do?
Tsar: I tried to send him away. Sonny wouldn't hear of it.
Tsarina: He had the power to stop the bleeding.
Tsar: Once I banished him to the Crimea. Then Nicholasha tripped.
Tsarina: He started bleeding. I telephoned our friend, come quickly.
Tsar: A creature that came out from under a rock.
Tsarina: It was God's will. Why?
Tsar: More dead leaves under the bed.
Tsarina: What had I done to deserve His wrath?
Tsar: Sonny blamed herself.
Tsarina: All that mattered was that our friend could stop the bleeding.
Tsar: The price was enormous. Through the child this strange human being came to dominate our lives, and the throne. Who would've guessed it?
Tsarina: What else could a mother do? He was my son, heir to the throne.
Tsar: It was bizarre. Frankly, everything around me was strange, less than I expected, cabinet ministers pulling in different directions.
Tsarina: I couldn't turn my back. I felt responsible.
Tsar: Father never showed me the art of governance. I was never privy to the inner workings of his cabinet. It was all a mystery. I could never understand why anybody would want to kill us. Then father died and all eyes turned to me. Well, it was a

daunting moment. I discovered a disingenuous ministry telling me one thing and each other something else. Sonny was right. I should've been firm to the point of . . . I, ah, refuse even now to say it. Ruthlessness was never part of me. I liked to build model boats, dress up to review the troops. I never had the stomach for leadership, the necessary–

Tsarina: I wanted to pore my will into you.

Tsar: Leadership takes a great actor with the skin of a rhinoceros and the heart of a wolf. I could trust no one, Alexander. May I call you Alexander?

Kerensky: Of course, your highness.

Tsar: O, let's dispense with that formality. No need for it now. (Beat.) I confess much to my regret that I had no idea things were so bad. You know first hand that leadership requires trustworthy administrators, but where do you find them? I put together a cabinet and couldn't trust any of them. The trick in life is to know who is lying, and who is telling the truth. (Gradually fading away.) My benevolence was taken as weakness. The people loved me and I loved them. I tried to be a good shepherd; really I did try, but my wife, my son, and that maniac Rasputin—slava bohu! (O, God!) I should've been stern, tied an anchor around them all and dropped them in the Baltic Sea, starting with my cabinet ministers those sycophantic self–indulgent liars. O, I am glad to be done with it.

Tsarina: You don't mean that, Nicky.

Tsar: Can the stupidity of leaders ever be forgiven?

Kerensky: Not when it causes death. (Lights up Trotsky at his desk.)

Tsar: I should've been a sailor on the open sea with nothing but sky and the ocean slapping the prow, the briny wind on my cheeks and lips, clean, uncontaminated. I tried to act on behalf of the people. (Fades into BG.)

Trotsky: (Crumples paper.) The Romanovs acted despite the people. Even an idiot can think himself justified while perpetrating disaster. Law and trust binds society in the great bargain where individuals give up certain rights, instinctual rights for group protection, which in turn obeys the laws, and its members live without fear of molestation. Perhaps, in a sense, the man is innocent. Three hundred years of Romanovs set the table for him. He was born and bred believing in the divine right of kings. Of course the first king who thought it up knew it was voodoo nonsense to fool the gullible people. Bah! (Beat.) In the middle of a world war Russia was suddenly swept up by a sense of freedom and liberation from the most elementary restraints essential to every human society. *Life was naked once again, unbridled, and doing as it damned pleased.*

Kerensky: Allegiances turned on a kopeck. One minute you were *this* and the next *that*. To this day, nobody can define any of it. Crime soared. Soldiers relieved officers of their swords. Everywhere it was, "Comrade this, Comrade that, but underneath deceit and betrayal.

Trotsky: After the October coup we had to find ways to implement policies, and reconcile differences—the inevitable struggle between the ideal and the practical.

Kerensky: You were an insider and Lenin's heir apparent. What happened?

Trotsky: The members of the Central Committee and the Politburo were preoccupied with petty jealousies and vying for power while simultaneously consolidating our gains, and working to revive the economy in order to establish a socialist–communistic state. What went wrong occurred in subtle degrees like a slow moving fog, one thing leading to another until we were overwhelmed, inundated by the thing we abhorred. The divisiveness and squabbling between members of the inner circle played into the arms of the insipid Stalin. Russia became the first paranoid state in modern history. An ESOP lingo emerged, or opposites. Questions were answered in parables. To agree was to disagree, maybe. A policeman stopped an elderly Jewish lady. *Identification papers, please.* While checking them he says, *and how are you Mrs. Schwartz?* She says, *Nu? How should I be?* (Lights up on Stalin smoking a pipe.)

Stalin: Bread is bigger than democracy but ego is bigger than bread. Around me you'd better know which side it's buttered on. Even so I'll flip and flop just to watch you squeal and squirm and then feed you to the dogs. Intelligence and character have nothing to do with leadership. It takes cunning and audacity. Lenin's old guard consisted of internationalists versed in languages, and philosophy. Great talkers. But this old country boy dispatched all of you. You, you, and you! (Pounds chest like gorilla.) I whipped Russia into the 20th century. Sukhanov called me *the gray blur in the background,* but never so far back that I was out of touch. He paid for it. By 1930 he fell off the map. By 1938 Lenin's old guard fell off the map, too. It was spearing fish in a barrel. Lenin taught me: *time waits for no man.* I encourage talent in order to destroy it. I kept one rule of thumb, *when in doubt kill the man and you kill the doubt.*

Kerensky: Trotsky, what happened to you personally?

Stalin: Me, that's what happened. (Sits in rocker "dock" behind scrim.)

Trotsky: I dislike the way power functions, its tendency to alienation of the people, its transformation into a brute hierarchy sitting on people's heads. I became disenchanted seeing our leaders turning into autocrats. Privilege and hierarchy during war are necessary. I enjoyed the brotherhood of ideological revolutionary movements, but along the way that camaraderie of single-minded purpose disappeared. Officials had villas, dachas, cars, enjoyed privileges without moral discomfort or the need for pretext. In Bolshevik hands power became arbitrary and unscrupulous. Next thing we were in conflict with the classes that supported us: differences in the way things were handled, opposing opinions on all matters: food distribution, etc. The members of the Constituent Assembly threatened to pull the Bolshevik Party down. So they turned a deaf ear to the people in order to survive. Then to have to squash the Kronstadt rebellion, our own people—it was the Kronstadt's fighting men and women who initiated the revolution. Perhaps we should've listened to them.

Kerensky: What about the farmers and collectives?

Trotsky: It bothered me when we turned our backs on the peasants and subjected them to economic hardship and police pressure. The cities had to be fed. We requisitioned food and materials by squeezing the people's last drop of blood as if they were strangers.

Kerensky: Lenin was out to build an assembly line society of mechanized people, human worker bees for the good of the queen, or the group. To Lenin, I say, *people are not things, made of gears, nuts and bolts.*

Trotsky: We were from villages, too. But we forgot that it was the backward poor suffering, beleaguered peasants, their sacrifices that helped overthrow the old regime. Suddenly, they became less than sheep herded into meetings, pressured to sell to the state at set prices. The distancing of those in power from the peasantry and workers was a subtle transformation of communism into an elite presumptuous, and condescending, which contaminated the best intentions, corrupted dreams and ideals, returning us to the baseness of brutes. One's sensitivity had to be hardened. One's sight narrowed, and hearing turned off in order to make the mind immune to truth, fairness, right and wrong, consideration and love. I tired of the killing. We had a chance to make a new beginning, to build a new society the likes of which the world has never known. To do it we had to dig down beneath mind-sets, beliefs that have been hammered into us for a thousand years.
Kerensky: You tried to force a square peg into a round hole.
Trotsky: Our aim was a society where no one goes hungry, where the fruits of labor are shared in common for the good of all. We saw the Tsar's power was slowly taken over by capitalist bourgeois landowners.
Lenin: It was the same old gang in a new suit.
Trotsky: The whole state apparatus had to be destroyed.
Lenin: Especially the old police organization.
Trotsky: Always the base for counter-revolution.
Lenin: Burn them down, lock, stock, and barrel so no phoenix can rise out of the ashes. (Cheers.) In its place men and women are to be armed in a "people's militia" made up of workers to take care of the general welfare and sanitation; each member to give one day in fifteen from work to do service in the people's corpse with full pay: merged with the army, bureaucracy and the new police. Such a militia would guarantee order and comradely discipline practiced with enthusiasm. We must end rule from above by the state and its agents and replace it with rule from below. All officials must answer to the people. If need be replaced by them immediately. It is essential to spread the system of soviets (Constituent councils) through city districts and villages. But, the bourgeois is organized. If we organize, too, they can never regain what we have taken.

Kerensky: I place in public record photographs depicting the Bolshevik notion of justice. The last photos taken of the Imperial Royal family in Ekaterinburg. (Snaps fingers; pictures appear on a screen: the Romanovs in mixed poses, happy, pensive, ending with them shoddily dressed, then gruesomely bullet riddled sprawled out on a basement floor.) Who ordered such an abomination of all that civilized people hold dear? Who? It had to have come from the top.
Lenin: They were a potential rallying point for counter–revolution.
Kerensky: Was it revenge against the monarchy for hanging your brother Sasha in 1887? Life is riddled with conceit, deceit, egotism and egoism. Few people give straight answers. Trotsky hated Stalin, Lenin hated me, I detested him, and Stalin hated everyone, especially Lenin's inner circle.
Trotsky: By comparison to them Stalin was coarse, had a southern accent, lousy debating skills, spoke one language; while they were educated, worldly, and spoke several languages. He was inferior to them in every respect save one. He had the street smarts of a savage, never forgot a slight, and was vindictive.
Kerensky: First of all, Stalin was anti–Semitic, but oddly enough Kaganovich, a Jew in his cabinet, outlived him. How do you explain that?
Trotsky: He was useful, amoral, a consummate bootlicker, and anti–Semitic himself, maybe a self–hating Jew who did whatever it took to survive.
Lenin: If only life could be played like chess with inalterable defined rules. In games like chess you know where you stand right away. It develops a feeling of justice even immortality, which comes from total involvement and an untainted sense of honest engagement. In sports generally one must play by the rules whereas daily life demands vigilance because people are deceitful self–serving improvisers. In sports you have a referee, but no such solid creature exists in daily life. Societies and religions turn innate fellowship into an odd camaraderie of thieves raping and supporting each other in order to rob each other. We're all guilty in this life; destroy each other one way or another. You want answers? There are none, only endless questions rising from the ashes of aspiration and childhood dreams.

Kerensky: Your saintly iconic image fabricated by the Party and swallowed whole cloth by the people belies reality. Lenin, the great dedicated Spartan revolutionary riding his bicycle to libraries to study books and deep think long philosophical–economic polemics by the canonized Hegel, Marx–Engel: *thesis, antithesis, synthesis; workers of the world unite, you have nothing to lose but your chains,* and all that intellectual guff, when in truth your nose was often between the covers of a bed. (Hooting.) Maybe that got you in trouble, eh? Your painful and protracted death, which I wouldn't wish on a dog, was described in an official Party statement as death from "cerebral hemorrhage" like your father before you. A logical diagnosis, but rumors persist of something more. How did you die?
Rabble: Cerebral hemorrhoids! Choked on a fish bone! Died in the saddle!
Mamushka: (Gavels.) Silence! Were you poisoned?
Lenin: In a high fever and delirium I may have suggested it to Stalin.
Kerensky: I doubt you had to tell him twice. To quote your reply to objections of Stalin being let into the party, *every man has his usefulness.*

ACT 3

Pending Arrests of Bolsheviks

Scene 1

Time: Early Summer 1917
Place: St. Petersburg

Coachie: At the start of the summer of 1917 Lenin and the Bolsheviks had begun to make headway, but then suffered a serious set back.
Mamushka: When you choose the start of a road you also choose the place to which it leads.
Kranksy: (Enter quickly.) Sorry. I had to slip away without attracting attention.
Trotsky: You've got ours. What is so urgent?
Kranksy: The people are being roused up. Trouble from Kerensky and the Provisional Government. Big trouble. This is a copy of an inter–office memo. (Hands envelope to Trotsky.) Kerensky claims he has proof you're German spies working in collusion with the enemy.
All: Ridiculous. Fritzie agents? Never. What proof?
Kransky: A signed statement from a returned prisoner Lieutenant Ermolenko,
Lenin: Did you see it?
Kransky: No. It's classified. Kerensky says it refers to a huge fund handled by Eugenia Sumenson–
Trotsky: Never heard of her.
Kransky: Connecting her with a Koslovsky. Also, he has bona fide letters from her to Furstenberg and Parvus. They're preparing orders for your arrest now. The front page of Pravda has been cleared and readied for print. It will hit the streets with the

afternoon edition. Kerensky is circulating the word in the street. Now I'd best get back. Good luck. (Exits.)

Trotsky: Is that fellow reliable?

Lenin: Yes. He's an assistant to the Minister of Justice Pereverzev, and a known radical lawyer. I trust him completely.

Trotsky: But if they suspect he's one of us the whole thing may be a ruse to throw us into panic.

Inessa: A court requires evidence not hearsay.

Lenin: That wily Kerensky. Step one trial by press.

Trotsky: The release is signed by one of our leaders in the Duma, Gregory Alexinsky.

Nadya: Ilych, this is serious with the earmarks of developing into a witch–hunt.

Lenin: I can defend myself.

Trotsky: In court, yes, but in the street–

Lenin: What time is it? Maybe we can stop the printing and issue a statement countermanding their claims.

Trotsky: Ilych, think a minute. Pravda is going to press now. It's too late. We can always refute claims in the press, but Kerensky's stooges will whip up the people, and there will be no reasoning once the mob starts moving.

Lenin: If the accusations are taken seriously.

Trotsky: "If?" It won't take much to arouse them. They are wide open to suggestion for months. Defend yourself, yes, but from underground.

Lenin: To hide is to admit guilt.

Trotsky: You can't defend yourself from the end of a rope. I say, disappear and fight another day. If necessary, I'll surrender in advance of the mob. Jail will be safer than the street.

Lenin: Nechevo (Empty—nechego.) O, beware of jealousy; it is the green–eyed monster, which mocks the meat it feeds on. Someone better speak to Chiedze at the meeting of the Central Executive Committee, and demand that the Soviet intervene to stop further publications of these erroneous allegations.

Inessa: My intuition says it's already too late.

Lenin: We must stop the bleeding.

Zverdlov: (Entering quickly.) What the devil's going on? Mobs are forming up calling for our heads. I barely made it here.

Nadya: Kerensky.
Kollantai: Spreading rumors about the–
Zverdlov: Sealed train. I knew it was a time bomb.
Lenin: I was hoping to gain a foothold before running it up the flagpole.
Zverdlov: They'll run us up that flagpole.
Street Voices: Spies! Traitors! We'll get you.
Trotsky: It's started. Pravda hit the streets?
Zverdlov: Yes. I went round about to get here.
Trotsky: A trial for treason makes great propaganda.
Lenin: Kerensky gets round one.
Nadya: Ilych, no trial.
Kollantai: It would be a fait accompli.
Nadya: There was no collusion, no commitments.
Zverdlov: Trial? You're joking? (At window.) We won't get five feet.
Inessa: There were and Ilych knows it. (Beat.) Free trip, release of German prisoners, if and when, etc. Shake hands with the devil he never lets go.
Lenin: It was never finalized. We must issue a statement of denial immediately.
Trotsky: It's too late for the afternoon edition. By the time the late one hits the street the damage will have been done. Better to issue a denial from a safe hiding place. There will be no holding back the mob, no justice but the rope.
Kollantai: There is no lynching law at present, or the death penalty, or hard labor, but only the risk of imprisonment.
Trotsky: In court, maybe, but the street is rash, impulsive.
Zverdlov: You're thinking crazy. I barely made it here. (Checking window.)
Lenin: A rather big "if" when it's your neck in the noose.
Zverdlov: All our necks.
Trotsky: Is there validity to these claims, Eugenia Sumenson, her connection with Koslovsky and her letters to Furstenberg?
Zverdlov: This is no time for chitchat.
Lenin: Kerensky, that hysterical windbag, hopes to divert public scrutiny of his government's failures, and I am the bogeyman.

He's a clever one. Had we seen this coming we might've taken the wind out of his sails.

Trotsky: On the face of it even I would hang us all. Well, maybe not me.

(Street voices, running feet: "Traitors! Saboteurs!" Banging on the front door.)

Lenin: One step forward two back. Adversity, Nadya, makes me fight harder. It makes men, prosperity makes monsters. Victor Hugo. (They exit as the rabble waltzes in singly, mixed couples Kerensky leading clutching arrest warrants.)

Kerensky: The chickens have come home to roost! By God! Cover the exits! Check every room and corner, under the rug, under the floor, between cracks, look for red under the bed. The "shock battalions" have been alerted. Arrest those German vermin playing footsy with Hermann!

Rabble Voice: Sir, the militia is out, troops, dogs, vigilantes, too.

Kerensky: Wundabar!

Rabble: Face footsy with Fritzey! Show your double face! We've a bone to pick with you Bull–shevik saboteurs. Traitors! Agitators! Provocatators! The devil in a worker's peek cap. The brass of those snakes in the grass. Hang their hairy asses! You'll swing in the wind. I could use a few deutchamarks myself. Shut up! Bunch of Bull–shevik artists!

Coachie: One thing more that was not there before but goes straight to the core. It came into play after that sealed train day. Massive financial aid from the Kaiser, surprised even Lenin living like a miser. Enough money to support subversive activities, publish party papers and propaganda. All doled out in a Byzantine warren of pseudonyms, and secrecy, a grotesque merry–go–round of fakers and double dealers. After Lenin arrived there were more secret agents in Pete than needles on a Christmas tree, with phony names and corporate titles, trading companies whose workers never knew they fronted subversive activities. Petersburg was full of enemy intelligence, and counter intelligence, multi–lingual double–dealing agents, some with allegiance only to their pocket books in a game without honor or ethics: a Chinese puzzle worthy of the high courts of intrigue of ancient China. Why not?

We Russians are descendents of the Mongol hordes. Sometimes I get inklings to plunder and ravish, and roll over people—riding a horse, swinging a scimitar. The devil be damned—burning, killing, raping from one village to the next accountable to no one.

Rabble: (Dancing joined by Mamushka.) Lenin to Parvus to Wilhemstrasse; Zimmerman to Furstenburg . . . who communicates back to Lenin–Furstenburg connecting Furstenburg to Berlin . . . . through Gustav Mayer's link between Furstenburg and Karl Radek reporting to Diego von Bergen, a German minister responsible for *Allocation of Deutchamarks* for political subversion . . . to support and sabotage, *subvert and suborn Russia's war effort* . . . Wilhemstrasse to Zimmerman to Furstenburg to Berlin and Gustav Mayer to Furstenburg to Zimmerman to Karl Radek to Diego von Bergen Get it?

All: No!!

Mamushka: Now the sequence in reverse:

Rabble: Berlin to Diego Von Bergen to Mayer to Radek to Furstenburg to Zimmerman to Parvus and back to Lenin. Hang 'em in reverse! Parvus contacts Wilhemstrasse, somebody named Zimmerman, who in turn connects to Jacob Furstenburg who communicates back to Lenin. Another link is Furstenburg and Berlin through Gustav Mayer's link between Furstenburg and Karl Radek reporting to the German one Diego von Bergen—the moola man. Minister for allocation of money to subvert and sabotage. God! I'm getting a headache. Is Lenin Jewish? On his mother's side two generations back. Pull his pants down and you'll see. If he's circumcised I'll kill myself. What's the difference? We have a Hessian for a Tsarina, a Tsar whose five point six percent Russian. The Kaiser's his cousin. Just yesterday I was milking my goat. You keep a goat in Petrograd? Where? Under my bed. What about the stink? The goat'll get used to me. As I squeezed for milk, I thought, one squeeze for me and 20 for Mother Russia. It's robbery. An inspector comes by demanding the last bit of food I had to feed my animals. Ok. Then he wants half of the last squeeze of milk from my cow. So I squeeze his you–know–what. Tfu! They kill a cow for meat and wonder why there's no milk. Tfu! Tfu! (Lights down and up on cameos delivered fast in and out of the audience.)

1

Zinoviev: We scattered and regrouped at Marguerite Fofanova's, Nadya's friend, in an old red brick tenement in the Vyborg district. Then Ilych and I in disguise went to live in Alliyev's apt, Stalin's future father–in–law. No place in or outside of Petersburg was safe. We could hear the hunt outside. Vigilantes, police, and Cossacks scurrying back and forth searching for Bolsheviks.

2

Rabble: Petrograd's a stone barn full of vermin and rats. Burn it. Naked people dancing on doors and windows. Disgusting! And no balls. They froze and dropped off. Filthy, blood sucking aristocrats! Tfu! Maybe there's food inside. Y'can't eat oranges off a picture. I hear Lenin and Trotsky owned serfs. We going to burn this place or stand around milking a dead cow? Burn it. The only way to get rid of rats. Maybe Lenin's inside under a bed. I've got a bed for him, a bed of roses. Mayer to Furstenburg to Zimmerman to Karl Radek to Diego von Bergen and now from the people back to you!

3

Kamenev: Stay out of Petrograd. The police are everywhere!
Lenin: I won't tolerate this! Let's seize power. We must light the way!
Sverdlov: Wait for the Congress–
Lenin: Whose future is uncertain? Waiting is a fool's game. Kerensky could succeed unless we act swiftly.

4

Kerensky: Comrades, if you oppose the looming threat of the Bolsheviks, if you disagree with other minority parties, I say, join with me and together we shall go forward and win the battle for a better tomorrow. My strategy concerning the Constituent Assembly is that Russians have never before voted on a vast national level. I want a Pre–Parliamentary temporary assembly in which all sections of the community are represented and will sit until elections are held.

5

Lenin: It's a tactic to consolidate his forces. It must be sabotaged! If the Central committee doesn't act they'll face dire punishment! The situation is critical. We must strike before Kerensky gets too strong. Overthrow him now. Otherwise I resign from the Central Committee and free myself to appeal to the lower party ranks. If we wait for the Congress of Soviets and let the moment pass, we will destroy ourselves, and lose our last chance for power.

6

(Petrograd meeting under hanging lamp at Galena Sukhanov's apartment.)
Zinoviev: Where's your husband?
Galena: Working late. I suggested he sleep at the office.
Sverdlov: He knows we're here? Good. The front line troops are behind us.
Uritsky: The situation is different now. You sure about the troops?
Zinoviev: On this I'm with Kamenev.
Lomov: You, against Lenin?
Zinoviev: A coup now is premature.
Uritsky: No. The time is ripe.
Zinoviev: Fail we lose everything.
Coachie: Stalin used this point of opposition to Lenin as one of the reasons to condemn Zinoviev and Kamenev in the purge trials of the 30's.

7

Rabble: The Bolsheviks can go to hell for my money. In rubles or deutchamarks? They meant well. The road to hell is paved with good intentions. In the end we all get our just deserts.

Scene 2

Vigilantes: Swines! Through Germany with Kaiser Willy's blessings. Traitors! Scoundrels! Lenin, Trotsky, Zinoviev, Sverdlov where are you? Show your face I'll smash 'it! That sealed train sealed your fate! There's Lenin sneaking out of a doorway. Quick. He's headed to the woods! (They tackle him.) Pull off his wig! Can't. It's real.
Man: I'm a farmer from the Volga
Vigilantes: You're far from home, comrade. Why?
Man: Visiting my sister.
Vigilantes: Your name?
Man: I can't remember. Um, Gregory Gregoriovitch, that's my name.
Vigilantes: His papers check out. Go back to your sister.
Man: Thank you so much. I have 10 children. Thank you so much. Where can I get some milk?
Vigilantes: We're giving you the milk of human kindness by not killing you. Ten children? Go! Before we yank out that wild hair of yours, widow your wife, and orphan your children. She could use a break. (Man exits.) He's got his own army. (Mimicking him.) Thank you so much. I have 10 mouths to feed. I'm just a farmer. No wonder the crops are small. Instead of the land he's plowing his old lady! Bet he doesn't know the difference! There ain't none. Sex n' farming, sowing n' reaping' are the same thing. Shh! Someone's coming. (A group runs by, followed by the officer cadet corps, an angry military Kadet Party chased by Cossacks.) Junkers! Cossacks! Don't get in their way! They want more than blood. They're angry over casualties to their comrades at Liteing Bridge.
(Allilyev's apartment.)
Lenin: We can't stay here. It's not safe. We're being watched, I'm sure of it.
Zinoviev: Allilyev, Lenin, Stalin, and I left the apt 11PM under cover of darkness and made for Noraya Derevnya to get the train.
Lenin: It's safer walking; cars are being stopped by patrols.

Zinoviev: Arrangements were made with Nicholas Emelyanov, a veteran Bolshevik, to meet by the Stroganov Bridge over one of the Neva tributaries. Allilyev and Stalin returned to the city. We took back roads to the station on the outskirts of the city, crawled under a freight car, waited, and then clamored onto the last coach as it pulled out. Ilych sat inside the exit compartment.

Lenin: No. On the footplate of the coach in case I had to jump off.

Zinoviev: It's dangerous, I said.

Lenin: Never mind. I'm good at holding on.

(Inside the train they play drunk; soldiers wander by; Lenin rolls his head to the train rhythm making it difficult to be identified as soldiers move on. At a stop boisterous officers exit a restaurant buffet, climb aboard singing obscene army songs, talking politics, and abusing Lenin.)

Officer: Who are you bums? (Looks closely at Lenin hunched shoulders, head bobbing in time with the train, bending lower and lower as the officer tries to see his face. Officers go.)

Zinoviev: Later, we hid in a loft, but were forced to leave by Cossacks scouring the area.

ACT 4

The Bones of Contention

Scene 1

Place: Public Forum at the Sidewalk Tables of the Pearly Gates Bistro
Time: Limbo
(Note: Kerensky denounces Lenin and Bolsheviks as spies.)

Kerensky: Let the Congress of Soviets convene. Places gentlemen. Thank you. I was furious on returning from the front. I had telegraphed orders, "arrest all Bolsheviks leaders" and they were disobeyed. I relieved the commandant of the Petersburg Garrison. I was even angrier with Pereverzev for releasing the embargoed Lenin dossier, which I can only blame on panic. It lost us the big fish, Jacob Furstenberg, and also Parvus who heard of the scandal while on his way to Russia, and turned back to Stockholm. I demanded the cabinet dismiss Pereversez. I was told it would've been premature to make arrests before an investigation. There was no one I could trust.
Aide: (Entering.) Telegram from the front.
Kerensky: What next? Thank you. Here. You read it. (Sits.) It can't get worse.
Aide: Germans attack. Major break through at Tarnopol.
Kerensky: Good God! Well, Heir Lenin, Vladimir Ilych Ulyanov, or whatever your aliases and incarnations, the people you claim to serve mean little to you except as stepping–stones to power. I accuse you of returning for the purpose of subverting popular support of the government; of collusion with the enemy; and undermining the army's will to fight for its country.

Lenin: You have prejudiced your case based on unsubstantiated news releases.
Kerensky: The old barrister of Simbursk is still alive. I bring to your attention a poem on the Lenin/Bolshevik legacy written by a Russian poet while in the "gulag archipelago". It's titled, Morons of the Revolution: *O, brilliant, you say? Yes. The best and brightest minds. Self–indulgent idiots! Revolutions in the end go haywire. Between the thought and its execution, the dream and reality, the practical and ideal falls the truth of what is, insipient weak–minded self–centered personal truth. Man, lame–brained dreamer in brute body, sipping hot toddy on the threshold to nowhere. Nothing wrong with revolution. Change now and then re–invigorates. New blood replaces old blood. New life pushes out old life. Even in the realm of ideas. Every second we stand on the brink of extinction. Is it time? No. Push on, old friend. Is it time? No. Soon, very soon. Half past the hour? Possibly. Sometimes life has to be forced, helped along to do in a minute what nature would do in years.* Lenin was one of those helpers. Where were you living before coming to Petrograd?
Lenin: Zurich to Petersburg by way of Germany, Sweden and Finland. The shortest distance between two points is still a straight line. In Zurich the latest news was always posted on a bulletin board Neuse Zurcher Zeitung at the lake. Based on tidbits of news exiles would build edifices of theory, which the next bulletin would crumble. (Lights dim, relives Zurich experience.) Nadya, I must get to Petrograd. I wrote Ganetsky in Oslo, asking him if he knew a way to smuggle me through Germany to Russia. Couldn't sleep last night, tossing and turning, my mind devising all sorts of travel schemes: find a plane to fly over the embattled frontiers, borrow a Swedish passport, and take a train through Germany to Sweden. Learn a couple of Swedish words.
Nadya: You might fall asleep on the train, dream of Mensheviks and wake up screaming in Russian, "Scoundrels!" and give yourself away. Unless–
Lenin: What?
Nadya: Never mind.
Lenin: Say it. What?
Nadya: Go by way of England.

Lenin: Yes. I'll assume Karpinsky's ID. He manages the Russian Library in Geneva. I'll wear a wig; go to England and then by way of Holland and Scandinavia. I've considered it from every possible angle. Karpinsky will procure in his name travel papers to France and England and I will use them going from Holland to Russia. Karpinsky for his part will of course disappear for a few weeks. I'll telegram him from Scandinavia when I'm safely there and he can come out of hiding. We'll pay for food and lodging, of course. Ah. Going through England would take too long and I might get detained. (Pacing; fuming.) No word from Ganetsky. I can't wait any longer. Zinoviev and I must get to Russia. Maybe we could find two Finns who look like us, pay them to stay undercover in Zurich for a week, and use their passports.

Nadya: Since you can't speak Finnish they should be deaf mutes. Let's take out an ad: Finnish Person Wanted, Must Be Deaf Mute Who Looks Like the Notorious Revolutionary Lenin.

Lenin: Oh, stop. Do I look notorious? I don't feel notorious.

Nadya: It's not a look. It's a reputation. Though at times your smile is scary.

Lenin: Really? How scary? Grr!

Nadya: Volodya, it's not necessary to force it. Just being you is scary enough.

Lenin: We're all scary, my dear, because we're unpredictable. Gr! (To audience.) The detestable centrist Robert Grimm made inquiries at the German Embassy in Berne and telegrammed the German Imperial Headquarters suggesting that the majority of Russian exiles in Switzerland are in favor of discontinuing the war. True. *There are advantages to be gained in helping them get to Russia. They'll add to defeatism in the ranks of the Russian army. It may be a bold stroke to end war on the Eastern front.* On the surface it was a sound idea, but could the Germans be trusted. They might set us up, shoot us, and send us on in wooden kimonos. My God! (Reflecting.) There could be collusion among the Anglo-French imperialists who encourage Milyukov and Guchkov to seize power in Russia in order to prolong the imperialist war. Those devils would conduct the war even more ferociously and stubbornly and slaughter new millions of Russian workers and peasants so that Guchkov may obtain Constantinople, the French: Syria, and the English: Mesopotamia. The revolution had been won only to have its fruits snatched away by Anglo–French conspirators and they are only waiting for the right time to reinstate the Tsar. It's all Russian roulette. Bah! Who knows? Even a thief has to trust somebody.

Kerensky: (From the dark.) Heir Von Lenin, you are a defeatist.

Lenin: I am not dismayed by the charge that by promoting revolution in my country I might provoke its defeat against Germany. Frankly, I would describe myself as a revolutionary defeatist, defeat of Tsardom would be the least evil in any circumstance. Socialists who do not share my view can go to hell! I say, no unity with those labor leaders who've become vile purveyors of cannon fodder to the general Staffs of Europe. *I call them traitors.*

Kerensky: Let's speak plainly. France and England were Russia's allies in the war. You, a well–known revolutionary, were fearful of being detained because of your radical views on the war.

Lenin: Radical because I disagreed with their imperialist thinking.

Kerensky: Are you a pacifist?

Lenin: Not in your sense of the meaning. I wage war on war. At the outbreak of WW I, I was taken aback by behavior of European socialism. On reading in the Swiss paper that the parliamentarians of German Socialism had supported the Kaiser's war, I refused to believe my eyes. I treated the report as a kite flown by the German General Staff to fool the working class into acceptance of the war. I became so downcast I thought of leaving politics. But I felt compelled to go on. We all have a mission in life.

Kerensky: *Compelled* and *mission* as in preordained?

Lenin: I am a pacifist who makes war on war.

Mamushka: War on war is still war.

Lenin: But my war is against usury, trusts, cartels and banks, the real unseen culprits and instigators of enmity between nations of comrades, the subtle enemies of decent human beings. I'd turn your imperialist war into civil war to liberate a people who'd forgotten the meaning of freedom.

Kerensky: Mamushka, Lenin was gambling the future with your life.

Mamushka: And his own. Get on with it.

Kerensky: Let's get back to the train.
Lenin: As you wish. You always had a one–track mind.
Kerensky: I stick to the point of destination and refuse to let your oratory skills and the glow of your messianic fantasies sidetrack me. The train made stops?
Lenin: Yes. Potsdam and Berlin to stretch the legs, and take on provisions.
Kerensky: Fuel, water, sauerbraten, wiener schnitzel, and a mail pouch full of deutchamarks. (Stepping into the light.) You met with High German officials?
Lenin: To make sure we were on the same page. It was not a people's war, but a capitalist–imperialist war between profiteering corporations, another lame excuse to kill and butcher innocent people who resist the robbing and exploitation of their land and their natural resources. In this war it's the people, both German and Russian, who pay the price with their lives. Russians only want bread, land and peace. You never answered that call.
Kerensky: What were the conditions?
Lenin: We were given the extra–territorial status of a Foreign Embassy, conditions on which returning exiles could travel freely through Germany.
Kerensky: Wundabar! How did you get Foreign Embassy status?
Lenin: We reached an agreement through intermediaries and envoys.
Kerensky: Does the name Victor Taratuta mean anything to you? Parvus, Jacob Furstenberg, Keskula, and Arthur Seifeldt, do they mean anything to you? No? He was your friend, president of a bogus corporation in Stockholm whose mandate was supporting you and your Bolshi cronies. I submit letters of correspondence between Lenin and Furstenberg testifying to their relationship in terms of money transferred. Furstenberg is the focus of most of the conspiracy evidence concerning German links with Lenin. Furstenberg was your errand boy who handled vital secret assignments. Do you know Keskula? No? He is the Estonian Bolshevik agent who spoke with you on numerous occasions, according to witnesses, and he fed money to you.
Lenin: I never took money from anybody.

Kerensky: In Bolshevik lexicon that means 'not personally', which is doubtful, but indirectly through bogus writing fees and Pravda subscriptions. 1907. Victor Taratuta—"The Lover" know him? No? He underwrote your Bolshevik Party by acquiring the Schmidt fortune of some "140,000 dollars." Perhaps it slipped your memory. To refresh it I place before the people's court as Exhibit A documents of a paper trail which I managed to salvage: Office of Records, Wilhemstrasse, dated, signed, and listing amounts of German money funneled to the Bolsheviks through The Parvus Trading Company. You received more than Foreign Embassy rights, Heir Von Lenin! The Party above all else. You would defend your cause to the last peasant. You made a deal with the enemy plain and simple to undermine the Russian war effort. How else could you and some twenty–five penniless émigrés travel freely through Germany when seats were at a premium and trains commandeered for transporting soldiers and supplies to the Eastern and Western fronts? German and Russian soldiers were at each other's throats while you received Foreign Embassy status from Zurich to Sweden. In addition, Kurt Eisner, the late Bavarian Prime Minister, was assassinated a year after the Russian Revolution. At the Berne Conference he exposed the war guilt of the central powers, saying, he had evidence proving that the German General Staff was secretly involved with Lenin, Trotsky, and the Russian Soviet Republic. This indisputable evidence smacks of collusion with the enemy. You are a traitor.
Lenin: Not me, you and your rotten Provisional Government—patronizing the people, feeding them defensive guff about the Fatherland. You humbug! The most direct root home was through Germany.
Kerensky: What did you promise in return?
Lenin: Nothing. It was understood that once in power we'd pull out of the war. The Germans wanted to focus on the West. We both played a long shot.
Kerensky: Why did you come back?
Lenin: To help protect against counter–revolution.
Kerensky: But instead of helping in a collegial way you set about undermining every attempt at law and order, systematically destroying Russia to achieve–, What?—*Rule from the bottom* in

which the lapel tells the coat, and the tail wags the dog. Poetry to beguile the ignorant.

Lenin: You incriminate yourself with elitist talk that presumes the people cannot learn. Societies like nature go through periods of change.

Kerensky: Kamo and Stalin, alias Koba, robbed banks to support the Party, which in your euphemistic lexicon was called "expropriation". They also stole matériel goods that were sold for cash that went into the Bolshevik coffers. It was *dirty capitalist money* but accceptable when it is to your benefit. Even the name of your party is based on a stolen quorum. You, Parvus, Jacob Furstenberg, Keskula, and Arthur Seifeldt are "expropriators" who lived on stolen capital. You see, Russians are not so stupid or backward that we can't add two plus two. (To audience.) Lenin made deals with the Germans: took deutchamarks to finance his *sealed train* trip, his Party, and subversive periodicals inside Russia. All along you have undermined our government, advocated capitulation in the war, and promotion of Bolshevik–Communism. You sought power by any means, power above even human rights. One fundamental truth has guided Heir Lenin: *the end justifies the means.* His protégé Stalin went further, "the end by any means. Stalin was Lenin's attack dog. Lenin taught the beast and then wondered why on his deathbed the man acted like a brute. Lenin was asked what is communism? He replied *Communism is the electrification of Russia.* I say democracy is the electrocution of Lenin.

Lenin: (Clapping hands.) Beautiful! The orator in search of the bon mot.

Kerensky: Your father was a certified nobleman that makes you an aristocrat. Your "family stipend" derived from mamushka's earnings off the sweat and blood of serfs. So don't pawn yourself off as a man of the people. It insults our intelligence. This proceeding is not comprised of the deaf, dumb and blind. At bottom, you are everything you denounce. On the one hand capitalists are filthy dogs abusing the people, but on the other hand you're not above using capitalist money for self–aggrandizement and Bolshevik aims. In 1918 the war was still on. You, Trotsky and the Bolshevik Party were fearful of Germany despite the Brest–Litovsk Treaty agreement, which gave no definite assurance Germany would honor its commitment.

Lenin: Let's not engage in a spitting contest.

Kerensky: The world had become too small and our dependence on each other too great to permit the luxury of ignoring enemies. Following the Brest–Litovsk Treaty of 1918 the Communist–Bolshevik Party issued a decree or propaganda thesis quote: *having taken over the government the proletariat and peasants led by the Bolshevik Party began peaceful reconstructing of the country, but the ousted exploiting classes started a civil war to regain what they lost and the imperial West fueled the struggle.*

Lenin: The revolution called for reorganizing the people into the first worker and peasant's Republic in history, which threatened the parasitical lifestyle of imperialists everywhere by endangering their profiteering, their money, and privileges. So they tried to put Russia in its place, by infusion of money and arms to beat us down. The people responded in a patriotic war to save what had been gained. Our energy was diverted from building a new state to fighting the combined armies of the imperialist beasts. The workers of the world were with us. Our victory would be their victory. Our success was a blow to imperialism.

Kerensky: I believe you've been obfuscating on thin ice.

Lenin: (Clapping.) O, such blowhard rhetoric.

Kerensky: The fact is that Russia was still part of the Entente in WW I. The allies were blocked by German subs in the Baltic Sea from building a storage base for Russia, and by the Turks in the Dardanelles. Vladivostock was too far some 5,000 miles away by a rail line through Siberia. So that left Archangel on the White Sea in the North Duma river delta, but it was frozen solid 8 months a year. So the allies built a port on the Murmansk inlet near the Finland and Norway borders. The Bolsheviks deceived everyone into thinking the civil war, which was the people's rejection of communism, was prolonged because of aid to the Whites by the West. But in fact it was internal division, the destruction of trust in our leaders by Lenin that enabled you to win. A railway had to be built to connect Archangel to the Russian rail system about 700 miles, which tied into the trans–Siberian rail system. England led all this work during the war when Russia was still a member of the Entente. Then the Russian Revolution broke out. I speak of the winter 1917–1918. The British had to protect the port and the supply root when the Russian Army fell apart—helped by Bolshevik agitation. The British supplied Murmansk and Archangel and protected them. Under the Provisional Government prior to your coup, the West had built up a great amount of matériel in Archangel for our use in the war effort. The matériel couldn't be moved because of rail breakdown. Tons of supplies necessary to the West's war effort piled up like precious metals were sacrificed for Russia costing money and lives. Russia never paid a kopeck for any of it to this day. Credits were given in lieu of cash. In 1918 in secrecy you stole those supplies—Excuse me, I mean *expropriated* it,—to bolster your weak position while simultaneously suing for peace with Germany at Brest–Litovsk. I also point to your callous disregard for the life of the people you claim to champion. Archangel needed food. Britain offered it in return for their supplies. They never received an answer. Food ships stayed in the harbor and rotted. It was more important to you to capture Murmansk than to feed starving people, whom you must've labeled bourgeois to ameliorate such cold–blooded thinking. Then in Murmansk you assassinated the naval commander, a Russian Admiral, a liberal who ran the base. Had there been no supplies in Archangel it's doubtful the West would've intervened in Russia. The West intervened to protect seizure of the supplies by your German allies as evidenced by your *sealed train* deal.

Lenin: The people were sick of the war. Had you heard them you might've stayed in office longer. You were booted out because you tried to divert the people's revolution back to bourgeois business as usual. The West was fearful of our potential, of our philosophy, and of our different ideas on governing. You say the West was protecting supplies from falling to Germany. I say it was an excuse to make inroads in Russia. They needed us and will always need us to balance out potential threats in Europe.

Kerensky: Let's speak plainly; you had no mandate! You bullied your way in with guns. In short, what you did to Russia the blood and horror you unleashed no amount of words can adequately describe. Now I ask you, would you have taken capitalist

money from the West if Germany took the offensive despite the Brest–Litovsk Treaty?
Lenin: It would've been impermissible.
Kerensky: In other words, no?
Lenin: No. The Germans had their reasons. We had ours.
Kerensky: Are we to discard your *sealed train* deal?
Lenin: Allow me to reiterate that it was important for me to get to Russia and lead the revolution. I insisted on special terms before accepting any travel arrangement. It was no secret then or now that I'd pull Russia out of the war. We first asked Milyukov and the temporary government to grant us permission to travel through Germany. Milyukov made no reply. We waited, but received no answer. Why? Were you a part of the Milyukov group that refused us permission to travel? I say yes. You deny me entrance and then presume to judge my methods. I tell you in all candor that Germany was the only immediate choice, the quickest way back. Fritz Platten, a Swiss socialist, acted as interpreter and go between. Parvus had to relinquish that job at a certain point early on because he and the Germans had a problem on other issues beyond me. I was glad of it because I wanted an unimpeded passage through Germany. The slightest trouble could've delayed or imprisoned us indefinitely. Now as then I fear neither truth nor false accusations no matter how damning. We should never spare ourselves to gain truth no matter the cost. My argument was not with members of congress as individuals, but with certain government policies, which were leading the people by the nose backward into the muck and mire of three hundred years of Romanov tyranny. You are grabbing at straws, anything to discredit me because you fear I will come between you and the people with the real reason behind your policies: the continuation of the old capitalist ways and reinstating that corrupt monarchy. I speak for the people. You speak for politics as usual. You fear me because I have the ability to put you in the street and out of a job, which you did not earn by plebiscite. I repeat the people did not vote you into office. Therefore, your words are hollow, the bombastic screeching of fraud. You've no legal position of authority to speak for the people let alone to pass judgment on anything. If you want a bogeyman look in the mirror. But open

those myopic eyes when you look. Instead of accusations you ought to reflect why you failed to satisfy the people's demand for peace, bread and land. You're the bugbear who sang the same old tune with different lyrics as self-serving as the old monarchy. Get it straight. The people did not want war, or prevarication just bread and land. Crooks and swindlers fear truth. A man at peace with his conscience has a clear face.

Kerensky: (Clapping.) Wundabar! I'll be even plainer. German contacts, agents, and saboteurs inside Russia had all but dried up. Who better to subvert the monarchy than a notorious revolutionary? Let Lenin return to weaken army resolve, oppose the Provisonal Government, and the monarchy. If there is a coup and Lenin comes out on top he'll be in our pocket.

Lenin: One thing was clear to me. History would not forgive us if we failed to get back and assume power.

Kerensky: I call on Zinoviev. Where are you? Ah, there you are. Tell us what was discussed in the Central Committee concerning Western aid?

Zinoviev: Allied aid had been debated in the Central Committee of the Russian Communist Party. Principles were at stake. Should a workers' government take money and supplies from dirty war-mongering capitalists? Lenin was elsewhere at another meeting. He was sent a note asking his opinion. He replied in a note, which became famous at the time. I have a copy in my possession. The question from the committee was, *aid or no aid?* Lenin replied, *I request that my vote be added in favor of accepting potatoes and arms from the bandits of Anglo-French imperialism.* The vote was in favor of such aid.

Lenin: Necessity breeds strange bedfellows. In any event nothing came of it. If asked under normal conditions I would offer a categorical no, but not in matters of survival. I'm not suicidal. I know when to compromise. Let me say to Inquisitor Kerensky that your mistake was being a defensist in league with the old bourgeoisie. What can be lost now by telling the truth?

Kerensky: Whose truth? (His aid enters quickly, hands him a note.)

Lenin: The objective kind. Listen, you old stick in the mud, the game is over. I was never for war. Support came to me for the sole purpose of releasing the Russians from bondage to an outmoded regime.

Kerensky: Let's not fiddle in the doorway. You were subsidized by deutchamarks through the Parvus trading company, a front for money laundering. So technically, you didn't take money directly from a German, but a courier is on his way from Germany bringing documents linking you to Kaiser Willy's aides. You won't wiggle out of this one so fast. (Reads note.)

Lenin: The burden of proof falls on the accuser not the accused.

Kerensky: True, very true. (Downcast.) Unfortunately, my source was arrested at the border, and the papers confiscated.

Lenin: Comrade Kerensky I tire of fatuous hindsight. Make your summation, go sit in the corner, and don't speak about what you can't prove.

Kerensky: We shall see what can or cannot be proven.

Lenin: What I am, what I stand for has never been a great secret. I was against your filthy capitalist war. Your Provisional Government policy is the traitor, peddling old wine in new bottles, and singing the same old imperialist songs. You're a jumpy, hysterical fellow. I take it you've played your final card and therefore, permit me, the accused, to rest your case.

Kerensky: In May of 1917 the revolution had taken a breather. At the time the Bolsheviks were outnumbered 20 to 1. After the monarchy fell I was Secretary of the Provisional Government. I tried to be a voice of reason. *No vengeance!* I cried. *Let's not sink to the enemy's level, but aspire to something better.* I became Prime Minister, was driven out by the coup, and barely escaped. My interest was Russia. Lenin would use her for world domination. Russia didn't matter to an internationalist. They are like the gypsies and separatist Jews living among us yet apart, gathering wool for themselves. The rest of us can go to hell. In those hellish days lives were swept away in seconds. In the grand sweep of things often important revealing information is lost. At first the people were drunk with freedom. The veneer of civilization gave way to the beast within. What was the secret to Stalin's power, his longevity?

Trotsky: Stalin understood intuitively that the more intellectual one is the less likely is he to kill. Stalin's appetite for blood grew on what it fed. I have often speculated on the secret to power. To Stalin it's duplicity, fear, terrorism, killing and periodic purges. While the rest of us worked to set up a new government, dislodging an entrenched establishment dug in for years with an autocracy replete with decadence and rife with bureaucratic skullduggery, pay–offs, and complaisance, which by definition sums up the petty bourgeois, Stalin was busy undermining our work. The man had no illusions about justice and the ideal state. But then what is justice to a throwback who sees the gavel as a cudgel? We like to think there is justice in the world: that good conquers evil despite the preponderance of evidence to the contrary. To keep our sanity our intelligence tells us there ought to be order, that there must be a rationale to the universe. Yet the facts are otherwise. So the mind creates hope; tells itself a good story, a nice lie, anything to mask the truth that we are utterly disgraceful creatures unquestionably alone, and quite mad. We are never more than a step from the abyss.

Stalin: In a capricious world the best defense is an offense without rhyme or reason: love through fear; create conspiracies, eliminate all threats real and imagined, rule with terror and fear, keep everyone off balance and fearful of each other, divide and conquer, poison the well, use people's vanities against them; and periodically have a good purge. I was willing to strike first without mercy or remorse.

Kerensky: The monarchy crippled the country. Lenin broke its back. Stalin demoralized it. It's a wonder Russia is still standing. How could you do what you did to your country?

Lenin: The real question then and now is how to get out from under oppression by the ruling class, not merely in Russia, but in the world? We were out to stop capitalist world domination and exploitation of people. You decry the harm we created, but millions died and continue dying under capitalism. We succeeded by force, each of us struggling in his or her way, but then we fought each other, and that was ruinous. In America Lincoln freed the slaves by proclamation, yet, they are still struggling for civil rights. Money, usury, capitalism breeds separatism, insensitivity, and class distinction. With money we think we're buying a piece of immortality.

Menshivik: (Rising.) My name doesn't matter only what I have to say. You can believe me or not. Stalin's period was a time of "terrorized silence," of joyless days and sleepless nights. Fear to speak out against injustice forced truth underground and began a full–blown age of lies, of opposites, of the anti–phrase, of symbols and metaphors that meant something other than what they appeared to be. The time of silence, closed doors, closed minds looking the other way became a way of life in Russia for decades. We are used to the lie. It came as a need to survive, to get along. Russians lied to protect themselves and their loved ones. The lie was a constant companion, and so when a thing was said we looked below it to the possibility that its opposite was the true meaning. One thing was said and another meant. One developed a 6th sense cause your life was at stake. Double meanings and opposites—smiles and silence hid the suffering and anguish.
Stalin: While they argued over minutiae I stayed back, waited, and when the time was right I stuck the knife in and solved all problems. Decision without hesitation regardless of severity was my formula, and paranoia my ticket. Kill all initiative. It spells danger. Innocence and guilt are meaningless. Man is the problem. He is dangerous, and unpredictable. Kill him and kill the problem. I delighted in creating joyless days and sleepless nights.
Lenin: Our values are misplaced. Competition instills a sense of failure, of inadequacy, of falling short of the mark. Cooperation is ultimately more valuable than competition. There is more good in a farmer cultivating the land than in all the kings and queens of the world. Krupskaya was right. Competing promotes elitism and destroys the possibility of a wholesome society . . . The mis–use of public trust is what gives a political system its bad name. Systems are inanimate. It is people who are responsible for the way a political system is administered. A good dictatorship is better than a bad democracy. The idea of government is simple, but the realization of it is not. The tendency to venerate Lenin speaks more to man's need than to my worth. In the Marxian–Lenin doctrine is the germ of Jesus Christ saving mankind.
Kerensky: The difference here is that the people were crucified. You were a "savage doctrinaire," and passed it on to Stalin, your protégé. Come. Tell us. Let's be candid in this last throw of the

dice. I announced sweeping program reforms, guaranteeing freedom of the press and assembly, a general amnesty, an immediate convocation of a Constituent Assembly "on the bases of universal, equal, direct and secret suffrage. And formation of a people's militia to take the place of the secret police, who were disbanded."

Lenin: Promises, only promises! But I admit that freedom gave latitude and scope for action. I said, "Make use of these relative and incomplete freedoms in order to agitate for a worker's government, which will give peace, bread and freedom to the people. Your government was unable to do it because its members belong to the landowning and capitalist class who would corner the bread market and sell it at their own profit and who were in league with the foreign imperialists who profited from the continuation of the war. I'll speak even more plainly. You did not have a grasp of the real situation. We sought no alliance with other parties. We reserved for ourselves the right of complete freedom of action, and began a program of massive agitation.

Kerensky: What about your faults? You saw conspiracies everywhere because they were the sorts of things you would do. There were no conspiracies to exchange one monarchy for another. People rose up suddenly and all the populace took part. My government represented and was responsible to them.

Lenin: (To audience.) The existence of the Petrograd Soviet of Workers' and Soldiers' Deputies indicated to me that a second more powerful revolution was highly possible. The Soviet of Workers' Deputies, the organization of the Workers' government in embryo—represents the interest of all the poorest masses of the population, i.e., nine–tenths of the population, which is striving for peace, bread, and freedom. The Provisional Government will ultimately have to bend to the will of the workers' government getting its power from the Soviets of workers' Deputies, and it's a stepping–stone from the new government to the dictatorship of the proletariat.

Kerensky: (To audience.) Lenin deliberately incited the workers to cripple the Provisional Government while it was taking its first steps.

Lenin: History was unfolding before us. It was as if an all powerful director had cued the masses to run in a certain direction, and on a vast scale accelerated the course of history, produced a crisis of unprecedented intensity, and the people swept away three hundred years of Romanovs. The story of God, of Jesus rising, the mystery surrounding all the profits . . . these are wilderness stories, man looking out into darkness for a place to hang his hat. Call it love, a yearning, willfulness, presumption, or senseless lamentation. Paradoxically, we have a need for truth: a notion of right and wrong. Does it extend into the universe? I can't say. Our quarrel is not with the universe, but how best to live in a temporal world. Exploitation is not the answer. The real enemy is egoism, the self–seeking exploiting class of capitalist dogs! We stand in the vestibule of the great era of *international socialism*. If death must come, if each of us is to die, then the fight worth fighting is the fight that liberates mind and body from oppression and exploitation. This is that glorious time. The people at last have been vindicated. In your quiet moments do not be afraid. Take heart. There is much left to do. We are the crest of a new world order. What is to be done? I call out to you from the bowels of the earth: destroy the whole state apparatus, especially the old police organization for they are the bases on which counter–revolution always wheedles its way back into power. You men and women shall take its place armed as a proletarian army charged with self–responsibility. Keep your guard up and your nerves steadfast. Don't let your triumph flicker and fade into oblivion like all the others. Do you want that? No! Keep vigil! Workers of the world unite! You've nothing to lose but your chains!

ACT 5

The Blue Notebook

Scene 1

Time: July–August, 1917: The Hunt For Lenin.
Place: A backwater farm across from Lake Razliv bordering Russia.

Coachie: In the summer of 1917 three years into the Big War the Bolshevik Party was at its lowest ebb rocked by arrest warrants issued by Kerensky's Provisonal Government accusing them of collaboration with Germany. Many Bolsheviks were imprisoned or shot by police, Cossacks, soldiers, and vigilantes. Trotsky, Kamenev, and Lunacharsky were arrested. Lenin and Zinoviev disguised as Finnish day laborers were hiding in a hut on a farm in the Finland meadows and marshes, a backwater place near Lake Razliv outside Petersburg, while a footloose Stalin passed messages between everyone.
(Zinoviev prepares tea; Lenin thumbs a newspaper.)
Lenin: The death penalty's about to be reintroduced.
Zinoviev: Here?
Lenin: In the army. A telegram from General Kornilov reads like an ultimatum. He says, "An army of maddened ignorant people not protected by the authorities from demoralization lost all sense of dignity and is retreating. The revolutionary government should stop this flight and wipe away the shame, or the course of history will bring other people who will remove the dishonor while destroying the achievements of the revolution and will not bring good times to the country." I detect a hidden threat. Interesting. The fool is even more trenchant. "After my *whole life* from my *very first breath* has been in devoted service to my

country, I now say that the fatherland is in mortal danger. As a temporary measure it is essential"—He doesn't dare tell the whole truth. The prevaricator! Devoted servant of the people! " . . . made necessary by the exceptionally desperate situation the introduction of the death penalty and drum courts martial into the theatre of military operations." That's serious stuff . . . a government decree reintroducing the death penalty signed by Kerensky, how characteristic of that windbag. Sounds better to the masses to say 'revolutionary' courts. The equally horrible Boris Savinkov the novelist terrorist supports Kerensky. "Death to those who refuse to risk their lives for country, land, and freedom.' Ultra revolutionary words full of rot.

Zinoviev: There is no land and no freedom.

Lenin: The leaders of the Plenipotentiary organizations of Russian democracy . . . blah, blah . . . the report of the joint meeting of the Central Executive Committee of Peasants' Deputies. Kerensky' says, "The government will save Russia and forge its unity with iron and blood." Such big talk from a little man, "iron and blood, should arguments of reason, honor, and conscience fail." That's a sly hint at us. Arrests, murder, foul slanders are considered arguments of reason, honor, and conscience. Nikolai Chkhiedze joined in promising full support of the Provisional Government. Kerensky embraces Chkhiedze with a kiss. How they love to kiss each other! History should take note, that in bringing back the death penalty, the petty bourgeoisie liked kissing one another. They kiss, you die. All is forgiven. Mr. Fyodor Dan tables a resolution in connection with the death penalty, which demands that you and I be brought to trial. This is the same Dan who brought into Russia four years ago a double–bottomed suitcase from Munich with my book, "What Is To Be Done?" Which he praised to the heavens, which then and now proclaims our goals: a socialist revolution. O, the twists and turns of history. O, troops are arriving to crush us. Not here, in Petrograd. The 177th Izborsky Regiment, the Vendensky Regiment, Kolts' 9th Command with machine guns, the Third Non–commissioned Officers' School. Already in Palace Square is the 14th Mitavsky Regiment paraded in full battle order and was met there by–

Zinoviev: Kerensky in his underwear kissing a picture of himself.

Lenin: Viktor Chernov, the socialist revolutionary leader, and the government's bourgeois minister. Things are headed toward Bonapartism.
Zinoviev: Toss me the blanket, please. Thanks.
Lenin: Save a corner for my feet. (Silence; reading.) You asleep? Captain Zhuravlyov claims the Soviets can't handle state affairs. He wants the death penalty at home and at the front, and including civilians. A Cossack Lieutenant goes one better. Russia needs a surgeon, a military dictator. Ha! Such fairy tales. Headline: Where is Lenin? It says, "Lenin was seen in Paris cavorting with a Swedish Music Hall Girl and a prima donna of the Bouffe D'Ete–" Kamuska. (Gossip) Bah! Yesterday I was in Sweden. Tomorrow maybe I'll be in London.
Zinoviev: Send me a post card care of Lake Razliv.
Lenin: I've been seen in two places at once. In Paris I displayed my protean proletarian self having reserved the number 5 private room in a fancy nightclub and "had intimate relations with his diva the Music–Hall singer Erna Eimusti, ordered dinner and champagne at 750 rubles, and tipped the waiter 75."
Zinoviev: Cheapskate. I hope she was good looking.
Lenin: Look here. "Lenin, Traitor and Saboteur was seen the following night in Berlin with two fraulines at a Rathskeller."
Zinoviev: I wonder how Nadya is taking it.
Lenin: Ka–muska! It is extremely disgusting and offensive to be accused of spying for Germany. Another article says we "have a private bank account with unlimited German money from which to draw on whenever needed to pay for lodging, and subversive propaganda." Where is this "famous" bank account full of free money? It's in their imagination. (Reads.) It seems Prince Lvov resigned and Kerensky is the New Premier, that hysterical dolt. "The Russian Lines have been penetrated by the Germans." "Thousands of Russian Prisoners Taken because of subversive Bolshevik activity among the rank and file." They call us "agitators" using German money to destroy Russian patriotism." Where is all this German money, I'd like to know? If we had it we wouldn't have been meeting in the basement of the St. Sergiua Brotherhood. The Mensheviks and social revolutionaries have joined Kerensky and the counter–revolution placing power in the hands of a military

clique that shoots down insubordinate soldiers at the front while it hunts down Bolsheviks in Petrograd. Behind this I smell that sinister Milyukov and the Kadets. Now the blind shall see and the stones speak the despicable slandering of political opponents. Je regret, mon ami. I should've insisted we take the power before Kerinsky got a foothold.

Zinoviev: No. We made the right decision to wait. The timing was off. Yet stuck out here in the swamps with all of that happening back in Pete makes me cry. Nothing but gloom and doom except for those couple of dates you had in Paris and Berlin. None of this gets you down. You're amazing.

Lenin: Gregorii, for an old pro at journalism you forget that news is often hyped propaganda depending on the paper and writer, a tertiary estimation of second hand facts, and not the reality of the thing itself. If you buy the premise you've taken the lure, swallowed the bait, and next thing you're in the fryer. Perseverance, comrade.

Zinoviev: Is that what we're doing in these marshes, persevering?

Lenin: Absolutely. Those who never quit but battle back in the end more often than not come out on top. I don't have a crystal ball, but I feel in my bones that something positive will come out of this. I will not surrender. I repeat it to put iron in your backbone. We will not quit the field without a fight. (Angrily.) You think me a funny, a clown?

Zinoviev: No. On the contrary, I'm thinking you're a drummer. Could've made a great salesman. You could sell water to a drowning man.

Lenin: We may be floundering now, but sooner or later the tide will turn, and even on us were we to gain power. Keep positive, comrade. It's the only way to prepare for the future.

Zinoviev: We've got a funny way of preparing for tomorrow.

Linen: In my mind we're already back in Petersburg and in charge. My plan–

Zinoviev: What plan?

Linen: Arms and force. One cannot make a revolution with manicured fingernails. Now let's change the subject otherwise we'll both get so excited and never get to sleep. All these newspapers, tons of rubbish, here and there a modicum of truth. We are the ones who know the truth, who are the originators and generators of reality, and not newspapers, which sit on the sidelines mistaking echoes for the thing itself. All they do is spread nonsense. They never go up against authority because if they did they'd be ostracized. Ah, smell that breeze. Good for the lungs. Breathe, breathe, comrade.

Zinoviev: I'm breathing.

Lenin: Compared to Siberia this is nothing.

Zinoviev: How we survived that place I'll never know. Well, we were young then. A Russian countess wrote a book about Siberia saying, among other ridiculous things—mostly kissing up to the British, that miscreants—people like us or worse, are mercifully consigned to Siberia not only to keep us from contaminating city people, but to colonize the land rich in natural resources for the good of Mother Russia. Well, it thrilled me no end to realize that I was not a felon but a colonizer. I had similar thoughts in the freezing cold staring into the bleak taiga when the temperature was–30. In fact during one blizzard I thought, Grigori old pal, how altruistic of you to be colonizing inhospitable Siberia the devil's back yard for future generations to enjoy. Ah, what a noble lad you are to sacrifice your youth, the prime of your life for the children of tomorrow and the likes of the Dutch East India Company. I began to think I was Daniel Boone of the Russian taiga.

Lenin: Good night.

Zinoviev: You sleep. I'm going into the woods to catch me a bear. You're welcome to come, but without your newspapers.

Lenin: Who wrote such a pipe dream?

Zinoviev: The widow of a former ambassador ingratiating herself to English society as belle of the belle arts who never did a lick of work in her life.

Lenin: Well, as one ex–colonizer to another, goodnight.

Zinoviev: There is a chill in the night air. Do you feel it? Bound to be a morning frost. The Sun will burn it off. I have an idea. Let's bathe in the lake in the moonlight.

Lenin: You go. Give me the details in the morning.

Zinoviev: Emelyanov plans to keep a cow, you know, come autumn. A cow's important, pigs too, sheep, and chickens, and horses, (Stretching.) and all living under the same roof. How do you sleep with all that noise?

Lenin: I'm having the same problem now with one critter.

Zinoviev: I nearly broke the scythe today on a stump.

Lenin: (Smiling.) We have a farm. My mother runs it with the family.

Zinoviev: Go on. Really? A farm? I thought you were town people.

Lenin: We were until my brother Sasha died, and our neighbors fell away one after the other. We became social outcasts. You see, the police were always watching. To be seen with us, even saying hello, marked you as a radical. So the neighbors stayed away out of fear. Finally mother decided she'd had enough, sold the house, and bought a farm with serfs on the outskirts of town. I managed it during the year I was expelled from Kazan law school. I did lots of reading and writing and once in a while I'd walk about to look things over.

Zinoviev: Did you know what you were looking at?

Lenin: Of course. A haystack is a haystack; a plow is a plow. Actually, I picked one of the smarter more experienced serfs to oversee the work and lead me around to look over things.

Zinoviev: Things? Ha, ha.

Lenin: And to point out the day's progress. I was tough mind you. O, yes. Give an inch as the saying goes. I used to crack the whip just to see the poor devils jump. If anyone failed in his duty I'd drag him up to the house and teach him to read. Some said they preferred the whip. Actually, they were all men and women of the earth—honest, genuine, not a mean bone in their bodies. I used to call them chefs of the earth. They'd feel the dirt in their hands, look at the sky, take a deep breath, and know when to sow and when to reap. It's for us, the ones lucky with an education to guide them, and see to it that they are respected.

Zinoviev: Absolutely.

Lenin: Therein is the crux of the matter. You'd think farmers would be praised and honored for feeding the world, but instead they are maligned by city numbskulls that think food grows on a store shelf. Make a note to remind me later if I forget to incorporate in our socialist policy that everyone should take a turn working the land at least once a month for a decent wage. It'll get the city folk out in the country, their hands in the dirt, fresh air in their lungs. Most importantly they appreciate mother earth who puts the bread on our table and the food in our mouth.

Zinoviev: And the farmer should work in the city, too. Probably the first day we'd all feint.

Lenin: Any enterprise worth a damn takes time to learn, time to build stamina.

Zinoviev: I like that "chefs of the earth." We're all chefs, aren't we, planting seeds in different ways?

Lenin: The whole world, Gregori, is mamushka's kitchen full of smells of home cooking, and her by the stove holding an admonishing wooden spoon. Everybody eating from the same pot and no one hungry. That's communism. We'll get there sooner or later.

Zinoviev: From here it looks like later maybe never.

Lenin: Then our legacy at the very least will point the way. Were there mistakes? Yes. But we made a start.

Zinoviev: Mooo!

Lenin: Hold your milk, you old cow. Sooner or later. Mark my words.

Zinoviev: Did you say mark or mock? (Yawning.) Peasant dreams, chef Ilych. (Silence.)

Lenin: The cow gives milk, the horse pulls the plow. Why beat them? Why skimp on oats?

Zinoviev: I saw a nasty farmer, you know. His horse had dropped on the road and he was beating the poor thing.

Lenin: That is the exception not the rule, comrade. Most farmers have the native intelligence to honor the land and respect their animals. Try to get those qualities from civil servants.

Zinoviev: Most they're out to lunch, or tell you "try the next window."

Lenin: Well, all that was long ago. There is a word for outdoor life. Invigorating.

Zinoviev: Despite the stars my bones tell me rain tomorrow.

Lenin: Let me stick my feet under a corner of your blanket. Thank you. I predict sunshine and happy news.

Zinoviev: You're the eternal optimist. We're stuck in these marshes, hunted by everybody, and you're nonchalant like it's all a walk in the park. Good for you. It must be tough going out here in winter when the winds blow. (Stokes fire.)
Lenin: It's not Siberia.
Zinoviev: True.
Lenin: I wore three suits and kept moving. I had a companion, a run-around, but she always came back to me.
Zinoviev: Nice body?
Lenin: Adequate.
Zinoviev: Did Nadya know?
Lenin: After she was exiled she arrived late one night and found us in bed. She kissed me and got under the cover with us.
Zinoviev: Nadya?
Lenin: In Siberia you do whatever it takes to keep warm. In fact, when we'd go hunting and separate she'd get excited, run about trying to bring us together. Ha. Idiot. It was Shu–shu, my dog. Nadya and I married in Siberia.
Zinoviev: The dog was best man.
Lenin: Best girl.
Zinoviev: Goodnight.
Lenin: Out in the tundra you always know who's the boss. I was fortunate because I knew how to make use of my time. Even now hiding like dogs in the wheat field I keep a positive outlook. It serves no purpose to cry over spilt milk.
(Silence.)
Zinoviev: Tomorrow we'll do enough to make it look good, to get that haystack higher. The exercise will be good for us.
Lenin: Kolya, I think it's his turn to bring provisions.
Zinoviev: And cigarettes.
Lenin: This little vacation is helping to get the cobwebs out of my head. When we go back they'll be no equivocation whatsoever on anything. Wherever there's an opportunity we take it no questions asked. All those years in exile and now this running and hiding—well, this will be the last of it, I promise you.
Zinoviev: In the morning we'll take turns cutting and hauling the hay. Break every half hour for a smoke. How many are left in the carton?

Lenin: Carton? You mean pack. We've got seven.
Zinoviev: Seven means a week at one a day. Wait. Seven altogether is three days. However, if we smoke half a cigarette a day they'll last–
Lenin: Ha. No wonder you're in charge of party funds. If we don't smoke at all they'll last indefinitely.
Zinoviev: Good thinking, Holms.
Lenin: Elementary deduction, my dear Watson. Doyle had it backwards. His reasoning was inductive not deductive. No matter. He always got his man.
Zinoviev: Except one.
Zinoviev and Lenin: The infamous Professor Moriarity!
Lenin: Yes. What's your favorite read?
Zinoviev: The bible, until I met you.
Lenin: We all grow up sooner or later.
Zinoviev: At night I like to curl up with a book on statistics. Numbers don't lie and everything adds up.
Lenin: In jail I spent a lot of time conjugating verbs.
Zinoviev: Ever think of conjugating women?
Lenin: That kind of thinking could kill you. I stayed with French and German.
Zinoviev: What's that book you brought with you?
Lenin: Turgeniev's Fathers and Sons.
Zinoviev: Gorky's good.
Lenin: Yes. But lousy at chess. The last time we met he seemed to have aged, grown cranky.
Zinoviev: How so?
Lenin: His views on socialism have a lot of heart but lack a sense of reality. In other words, he wants to make an omelet without breaking an egg.
Zinoviev: Who gets the blanket tonight?
Lenin: I just need a little section for my feet.
Zinoviev: You'll get no argument on that.
Lenin: This blanket is a good metaphor for communism: Everybody sharing under one blanket.
Zinoviev: I wonder. Is that possible?

Lenin: "On s'engage et puis, on voit,"—You commit yourself, and then you see. Napoleon.

Zinoviev: Right now what I see I don't like.

Lenin: Patience, comrade. Our doubts are traitors, and make us lose the good we oft might win by fearing to attempt. Shakespeare. You can go through life with only two books Shakespeare and Plato's Republic.

Zinoviev: Socrates could've escaped. Why did he drink the hemlock?

Lenin: Why did John Brown go to the gallows? He could've escaped. Why did my brother let himself be hanged? It was a matter of principle, an unwillingness to live a life of lies. Well, too much talk, Grigori, will get us riled up when we should calm down. See you in the morning.

Zinoviev: Scythe and tossing hay. All our work reduced to shit kicking. You know why? Principle.

Lenin: How much money does the Party have?

Zinoviev: Counting what's in our pockets, nothing. I thought you wanted to calm down? On which side of the zero would you like the decimal point? (Beat.) I admire you. I really do. You're resilience is child–like. Our backs are against the wall; make that the marshes, and you–

Lenin: Keep your head above the water. Ride the waves, Gregori.

Zinoviev: The water is shark infested, but all you see are angelfish.

Lenin: Crying over spilt milk is useless.

Zinoviev: What? You see a way ought of this? I don't know. At times you're so child–like. You can't just stop this business and say, I don't want to play anymore. Let's do something else. I feel like Hamlet in Yoric's grave contemplating my own skull while Ophelia's funeral procession passes by baring the coffin of the Bolshevik Party.

Lenin: Do not cudgel thy brains. I've always liked that expression..

Zinoviev: Don't start with that inky cloak crap. This German business has backfired with a vengeance. I remind you of a saying among bankers and businessmen: in any deal look around for a fool–

Lenin: And if you can't find him then it's you. Have you noticed, Gregori, so many stars. It sets you to wonder. There are more things in heaven than are dreamed of in your philosophy. I'm no sweet prince, nor do I expect flights of angels to sing me to my rest. Not yet anyway.

Scene 2

Place: Razliv Lake to Kuokkala, Finland
Time: July 22,1917.

(Shotman just arrived from Vyborg with red and blonde wigs for disguise.)
Zinoviev: (To audience.) Lenin directed the entire work of the Bolshevik Party from Kuokkala, Finland. The Leitezens left so we occupy the whole house. (Puts on oversized wig.) The Russian police are still looking for us but not in Finland. So we had a lot of freedom. The door was always open, a jug of milk and loaf of bread were left on the dining room table overnight, and bedding on the divan in the event anyone coming on the overnight train could eat, lie down and sleep without disturbing us. (To Lenin.) Have some hot tea, *Chaplinsky*.
Lenin: What's that? (Puts on a wig.)
Zinoviev: Tea. Have some, Chaplinsky; and leave a good tip.
Lenin: Gregori, this business is getting to you.
Zinoviev: Who would know in this wig?
Shotman: Who is Chaplinsky? (Lenin waves off question. Puts wig on.)
Zinoviev: Early use of the house by terrorists had certain disadvantages. We were sent books, letters, newspapers and food. Stalin sent Lenin a present of watermelon wrapped in serviette. Ilych started to open it. (Leaps at Lenin.) Stop! (Knocks him aside.) A bomb! It's ticking. (Tosses it away. Silence.)
Lenin: The ticking is in your head.
Zinoviev: A thin layer of poison spread over the paper–
Lenin: I don't plan eating paper.

Zinoviev: Turn a page poison gets on your fingers, you touch your mouth, and die. A sly trick invented by the monks to keep certain books from the people. When someone died they called it God's reward for sinning.
Lenin: Another reason to hate religion. Gregori, you're a font of knowledge, but you are starting to see assassins everywhere. Should we go about like paranoid ballet dancers fearful of stepping in bear traps or holes and twisting an ankle? (Cuts a piece of melon, eats, and fakes dying.)
Zinoviev: Not funny, comrade. Better to err on the side of caution.
Lenin: Cowards die a thousand deaths heroes only once.
Shotman: The wigs work. Maybe a slight adjustment. Try switching.
Lenin: What do you think?
Zinoviev: Kiss me.
Shotman: If you're going to Sweden wear the blond.
Zinoviev: I like the red. I feel better. What do you think, dearest?
Lenin: You're adorable. O, Shotman, before I forget. Next time bring my blue notebook. It is in the Timofeyech apartment. It contains years of research.
Shotman: Ok. I looked for wigs everywhere, side streets, alleyways. I had to join a theatre group to get them. I have a rehearsal tonight. I'm the butler in Chekov's The Cherry Orchid. The way those actors drink they should call it The Sherry Orchid. I'll show up a couple of times and then get sick. Now I'm going to take pictures for your worker's passes to the Sestroretski Plant. So far I've one name. I'm still working on the other one. Zinoviev, you're Constantine Petrovich Ivanov. Ilych, you are, let's see–
Zinoviev: That's not a Swedish name.
Shotman: You're mother married a Russian. Ilych, you're.
Zinoviev: Tor Bjorenson. Ha. Or Chaplinsky, his mother married a pole. (Goes to door, looks out.) No clouds. The sky's full of stars. That means a big workday tomorrow. Bigger than today.
Lenin: We'll do enough to make the haystack higher.

Zinoviev: I hope Kolya brings good news tomorrow, and cigarettes.
Shotman: (Puts on knapsack.) Be back in a couple of days with permits. (Goes.)
Lenin: If only life could be tied up in neat bows like a Sherlock mystery.
Zinoviev: These wigs would be a start. Open and shut. Case closed.
Lenin: We'd only skip to the end. Life is a mystery with minor and major bumps along the way.
Zinoviev: How do you see our mystery played out?
Lenin: Gregori, my gut feeling is always positive. If we knew the end in advance the road would bore us. Unpredictability keeps us alive and vibrant, my dear Watson. The sealed train has yet to reach its final destination. Time will tell. Out on the lake, a boat. Douse the fire.
Zinoviev: Look who's jumpy? Just shadows. They'd have seen the fire by now.
Lenin: Jump at shadows and the real thing will smack you in face. (Beat.) What a night. Has there ever been such a night? No. Not like this one. Every night is new. You just have to see it. Let your eyes grow accustomed to the dark and there a mystery unfolds with a million stories all quite different from the day. Are we day or night creatures, I wonder? Maybe a little of both.
Zinoviev: You and I are day people. Trotsky's a twilighter. Stalin's night. Sometimes in the middle of business his eyes will turn yellow. Ever notice that? They'll turn from gray to yellow–green serpentine. Seriously. Very spooky. They say, a poisonous snake bit Stalin and the snake died.
Lenin: Every man has his use.
Zinoviev: So bachevy. (Dog cold.) In Siberia they say *it's a three–dog night*. When it's cold you'd sleep with one dog, real cold two dogs, and bitter cold three. (Beat.) Ilych, you asleep?
Lenin: (Mumbling.) *Our doubts are traitors, and make us lose the good we oft might win by fearing to attempt.* We must keep body and soul together. Now, let's sleep. Too much talk will excite the mind and keep us awake. To be continued in the morning.

Zinoviev: You know what they say about you? Lenin and his principles are a pain in the ass.
Lenin: Really?
Zinoviev: No. But they will if we ever get back.
Lenin: Na vsekh ne ugodish. He who pleased everybody died before he was born.

ACT 6

Between Tauride and Gatchina

Time: Evening Oct, 1917
Places: A Bykhov Prison cell; Tauride and Gatchina Palaces.

Cameo

(Distant sporadic gunfire; explosions.)
Coachie: One October night in 1917 three men waited for news of an attempted coup: Lenin and Trotsky in the Tauride Palace in Petersburg, and Kerensky, Prime Minister of the Provisional Government, in Gatchina some 20 versts away. Both palaces had been the sumptuous marble playpens of the rich, a moot point now in the face of a bigger question, who will rule Russia? That summer pressure on the Bolsheviks eased up because of a sinking economy and an attempted military coup headed by General Kornilov. To stop Kornilov's forces from entering Petersburg, War Minister Kerensky issued weapons to everybody including the Bolsheviks. It was a matter of the enemy of my enemy is my friend. Kerensky shut down the transportation and communications systems, formed a civilian militia, opened the weapons armory, and distributed arms with orders to barricade the roads and bridges leading into the city. General Kornilov was neither popular with his troops nor inspirational enough to command their loyalty. His force dissipated at the out skirts of the city, the coup collapsed, and Kornilov was arrested.
(Bykhov Prison cell.)
General Kornilov: You politicians say one thing, do another, and we in the military pay for your mistakes with our lives. You shift allegiances like the weather. Well, we see through you disgusting politicians with your scams and pretensions, and it scares you. I stand up as a man and a soldier and call a spade a spade. Instead of admitting you've been found out you continue the old ways

attributing blame to others, circumstances, but we're no longer the trusting souls that you can knead like putty. We're fed up with lies, and spit truth in your face.
Coachie: The citizens returned their weapons to the armory, but the Bolsheviks kept theirs posing an even greater opposition to the Provisional Government than before the coup. Along side of this was the on–going war with Germany, a collapsed economy, no confidence in the government, and wide spread hunger. All of it contributed to resurrection of the dark horse Bolshevik Party and the second coming of Lenin. On October 27th the Bolsheviks made their move.
(Note: Squibs of dialogue in back and forth scenes independent of each other between the Tauride and Gatchina Palaces. Distant gunfire, explosions.)

Scenes 1 and 2

Time: October 26, 1917
Places: Tauride and Gatchina Palaces. Overlapping scenes.
(Lights up on:)

Tauride Palace

Trotsky: Ifs, buts, candies, and nuts.
Lenin: What?
Trotsky: If wishes were fishes.
Lenin: There would be no room in the ocean for fishes. If we succeed then the real thing starts. (Lights out and up on:)

Gatchina Palace

Kerensky: Perhaps I should've pulled out of the war. On the other hand–
Aide: We'd lose face.
Kerensky: Even so we'd have to contend with an anti–government element at home, and their counter–part in exile. Lenin sees revolution round every corner, behind every door, under the bed,

and even in the English tea bag. Well, there is merit in that. (They laugh. Lights out; up on:)

Tauride Palace

Lenin: Life keeps turning around. Yesterday the Razliv marshes, tonight the Tauride, and with the dawn who knows? Everything rides on Gatchina.
Trotsky: Kerensky may not have the stomach for this fight, or the backing.
(Lights out and up on:)

Gatchina Palace

Kerensky: Fighting on two fronts, three. Germany to the west, the Bolsheviks, Bundists, Social Revolutionaries and other splintered groups at home, Japan creeping up our back, and widespread hunger.
Aide: That's four, sir.
Kerensky: Four, five what does it matter? We're in an impossible situation. God! Where the hell is our reinforcement? They should've been here by now. A horse, a horse, my kingdom for a horse. (Lights out and up on:)

Tauride Palace

Trotsky: Any minute the doors might burst open.
Lenin: There will be no Siberia this time.
Trotsky: We should move closer to the window.
Lenin: It's a long way down. We could wait in the car in the courtyard with the motor running. (Explosion nearby.) Theirs or ours? They can only kill us once. What I liked most in Siberia were quiet winter nights, so quiet you could hear the smallest creatures breathe and stir beneath the snow. In the silence of all things one can hear the whispering of the stars, the creak of the earth's axis. It is ironic that a punitive sentence in Siberia had the opposite effect intended by the state. It became a meeting place for exchanging ideas.
Trotsky: A stew pot of revolutionaries arguing to keep warm.

Lenin: Ha, ha. It shows the depth of the monarchy's ignorance.
Trotsky: On the other hand they could've been merciless. What're the stars whispering tonight? (Beat.) Maybe Zinoviev and Bukharin were right. Maybe we should've waited. Maybe—(Lights out and up on:)

Gatchina Palace

Kerensky: It's more than Lenin. The country is tired of war. The economy is wrecked, food is scarce, and the opposition keeps undermining the people's confidence in us.
Aide: You did your duty, sir, as a loyal Russian.
Kerensky: Individuals and nations don't always make the right choices and suffer for it. They label me a "compromiser". I tried to steer a middle course between liberals and radicals to hold the country together when it was flying apart at the seams. My quarrel with General Kornilov—Well, I packed the son–of–a–bitch off to Bykhov prison for undermining my authority as Prime Minister. An army without government is dangerous. Better a government and no army than an army and no government. The army sided with Kornilov, leaving me without means to enforce peace. Then they betrayed him. Bah! Deceit is everywhere. The fool opened the way for the Bolsheviks who know very well how to exploit an opportunity.
(Lights switch back and forth quickly between palaces.)
Trotsky: Maybe we should've waited.
Kerensky: Betrayal at every turn.
Lenin: When night is darkest the stars are brightest.
Kerensky: They say I hate Lenin. No. I detest him.
Lenin: Kerensky's an hysterical windbag
Kerensky: That shabby puck, that monomaniac of socialism.
Lenin: Give me a fulcrum and I'll move the earth.
Kerensky: Where the hell are those troops?
Aide: The phones are down and trains have stopped running. Cigarette?
Lenin: The stage is set. The players are in motion,
Kerensky: It is never the people who cause trouble.
Trotsky: The outcome is anybody's guess.

Kerensky: It's always a crazy ten percent of wild–eyed lunatics hungry for recognition. The Bolsheviks are five percent of the voting constituency. Nothing anybody can do is right because they want the power. (Lights on Tauride.)

Tauride Palace

Lenin: While hiding in Finland Zinoviev and I were in the woods, took a wrong turn and got lost. I was furious. We were disguised as Swedish workers wearing field clothes with cheap looking blonde wigs under a stoker's cap. My wig kept slipping off. How would I explain to a stranger if in the middle of asking directions my wig fell off? It was ludicrous. In this Gregori was more positive and he assured me only our friends would know not strangers unaccustomed to seeing us. We had to cross a stream and Gregori stopped for fear of getting his hair wet. My anger at allowing us to wander off course got the better of me, my wigged slipped, and Gregori starts laughing. Hang me, he says, but don't mess up my hair. We had to stifle our laughter less we draw the attention of hunters or local farmers. We waded to the other side, quickly rediscovered the way back, and that night in my blonde wig I finished writing "State and Revolution".
Trotsky: This night is grimmer than your summer in the marshes.
Lenin: We can thank General Kornilov for easing the pressure on us. Kerensky had him arrested. If he's not shot he may be useful.
Trotsky: We'd have to re–build the military from the bottom up possibly enlist tsarist officers. They aren't all die–hard monarchists. While you were in Razliv I went willingly to jail. I was safer in prison than on the street at the mercy of roving vigilantes out for Bolshevik blood. Stalin kept a low profile in the suburbs with old man Alliluyeva and his family. (Distant rattle of gunfire.)
Lenin: Maybe that's our Georgian shooting the enemy.
Trotsky: Who knows? My impression is he sees enemies everywhere.
Lenin: Southerners by nature are suspicious. They've seen too many warring tribes passing through, and every regime drains them to the last drop. Show me an agreeable peasant I'll show

you a sly fox. It's the same for revolutionaries. The one time you drop your guard may prove fatal. (Beat.) It's going to be a long night. (Beat.) Siberia could've been worse. I moved about a good deal, didn't sit much, and made a point to never touch cold metal with my bare hands. One could lose a layer of skin trying to get loose.

Trotsky: At the first chance I escaped. Why didn't you?

Lenin: I had my books, my piano, and my wife. Nadya came and we married. There was lots of time to think and write and my sentence wasn't unrealistic. But, you know, it may seem contradictory, but I am a private man. I can only take society in doses, and then I must shut myself up somewhere to think and refuel. I'm not afraid of being alone. My writing blossomed. Being in jail keeps one's ass rooted with little distraction. Writing improves. What else is there to do other than go mad? Of course, had my sentence been extreme then—well, that's another matter. I dug into Marx, and Heine. Nietzsche reaffirmed my anti–religious sentiments. Concerning guilt and punishment, morality, if you will, Nietzsche said it was a dreamed up antidote to science and man's emancipation through learning, and designed to keep man from looking outside himself for knowledge.

Trotsky: In fact we shouldn't look at all and just suffer.

Lenin: Yes. To keep the people tied to religion and the coffers by way of guilt and punishment, redemption, and forgiveness.

Trotsky: For what, being born?

Lenin: Ha. I suppose. To instill guilt and suffering is to keep the people beholden. He calls the Garden and redemption a pack of bloodsucking lies without psychological merit, or reality. My sentiments exactly. The whole matter was born of cowardly instincts. A parasitic attempt to suck the goods out of people. A vampirism of subterranean bloodsuckers. I don't know which is worse capitalism or religion.

Trotsky: What frightens me most? The possibility that crickets might become carnivorous. Just a crazy thought. The sound alone disturbs me.

Lenin: Widget! Widget! Ha, ha. (HE shoves him lightly.) When you look back on this remember two little creatures waiting in the night rubbing their wings chirping about simple things

while their lives hung in the balance. Do you like hunting and fishing? When I'm not writing I do both. In Siberia I had a dog for a companion. Not such a bad life. Of course it's no place for schizophrenics. You could meet yourself coming back. In the taiga the air is pure and the quiet lets a man think. It suited me very well. I began to see in a different way. Appreciate the firs, larches, birches, spruce, and cedar trees. In summer I went for long walks, gathered huckleberries, bilberries, mushrooms. On a lucky day I'd catch glimpses of wild horses running freely across the steppe. My heart ran with them. And reindeer, beautiful, sudden and elegant, against the sun low on the horizon; they dart off after it. An old man told me that in the tundra reindeer carry the sun on their antlers. O, well. It's enough to make a man maudlin.
Trotsky: To me it was desolation; the climate unforgiving. Nature is cruel in the taiga, intractable summer and winter.
Lenin: There is wonder in its wide–open spaces, and animals. I saw a herd of hare. Really. The sweet padding sound they make individually is altogether frightening in a herd. I had to run for my life. Imagine? The local deputy writing home, sorry to inform you, but your son was trampled by rabbits. (Beat.)
Trotsky: The coup hangs by a hare. Ouch! How humiliating. To be trampled to death by a herd of rabbits. And now Kerensky, that pitter–pattering war mongerer. I still think we should've waited.
Lenin: There are three things, says an Islamic proverb that can never be taken back: the shot from a gun, the hasty word, and the opportunity missed.
(Lights out and up on Gatchina.)

Gatchina Palace

Kerensky: So the October coup by the Bolsheviks was not a quiet uprising of the people's will, nor is there truth in another myth that the West poured money and troops into Russia to stop communism. To bolster the Bolshevik's weak position, and to cover their theft of the West's food and military supplies stored at Archangel when Russia was part of the entente, Lenin invoked *nationalism* by issuing false propaganda that said Western money and troops were backing the monarchist whites. In truth, the West was primarily looking to retrieve its own sorely needed supplies, to keep them out of German hands. To back up a moment, growing social and ethnic unrest brought on by communal seizure of private land, workers taking over factories, and ethnic minorities claiming the right of self–government, dominated the summer of 1917. I tried a dictatorial approach, but admit not being temperamentally suited to it. I had no reliable power base. With every forward step I took two backward. All about me people pulled in different directions. I tried to steer a middle course between liberal and radicals. In the fall of 1917 public opinion had polarized. I quarreled with General Kornilov who was seeking to usurp my authority. The army turned against me. Now the field was wide open for the Bolsheviks to move without great resistance. Lenin made empty promises to every disaffected group, exploited the people's fears and vulnerability filling them with false hope. Land! Bread! Workers run the factories! To the soldiers he offered peace, to ethnic minorities, independence: and it was all tossed overboard once the Bolsheviks gained power. But they served the purpose of alienating large groups of the population from the government. That's the age–old trick, you see. Say whatever it takes to gain power then do as you please. In this atmosphere of chaotic allegiance one never knew where anyone's real loyalty lay. To Lenin, a man without a country, anything and everything was okay as long as he was in charge. He gambled with people's lives to put into practice an impractical vision of a communal world of drones where there is no place for individuality or artistic initiative. *The Revolution was a culminating point of wide spread discontent. Three years of war had exhausted the country. There was anarchy and dissolution in the military. Much of it brought on by agents–provocateur and Bolsheviks appealing to base instincts and fears that one was about to die for nothing, that the next bullet was for them. Why fight and die for a corrupt autocracy, a Hessian Tsarina, and the meshes of Rasputin? They planted thoughts of senseless death that went straight to the base fears of every soldier even the bravest. When the Revolution came they refused to fight. I saw the helplessness of Gutchkoff, Minister of War, in his efforts to stem the tide of anarchy and dissolution in the army and navy, the ineffectiveness of the Minister of the Interior in his struggle to overcome the anarchy in the cities and villages supported by revolutionary forces. I felt the decline of my own influence in the struggle against the Bolshevist demagogues because of the slippery dualistic policy of the Soviet in making its confidence in the government conditional on this or that point of theoretical casuistry. In March 1917 Premier Lvoff and the Minister of War released a proclamation that gave the men certain rights. Abolished the old salutations like Thou, Mr. General, Mr. Colonel, Your Excellency, Your honor, sir. After the Revolution the army stopped fighting and men refused to obey their officers. The instigators, German agents and Bolsheviks, had succeeded in stirring up the troops with subversive propaganda. The new Russia spiritually revolted against continued bloodshed. The subversive propaganda appealed to the dark side of a soldier. Their personal interest was above sacrifice for the common good. Reasoning can't change thinking that is felt in the heart and bones. Who can blame them for refusing to fight? I went about boosting morale. (Lights up in dugout at the front.)*

Soldiers: To the devil with the war! Let's go home! We've drunk enough blood!

General: I beg of you. Speak a few words. I've lost control because of anti–war agitators in particular a certain rabble–rouser. They need morale boosting.

Kerensky: Okay. (General blows whistle. Men gather around.) Soldiers of the Fatherland, how are you? (Moans.) Buck up. Your folks back home are proud of you. The bayonets of the would–be conquerors will not dominate us. Disregard poisonous German propaganda designed to undermine your fighting spirit.

Soldier 1 and 2: (To a soldier.) Now is your chance. Tell him how we feel. Before it's too late. What you're always telling us. Do it. (Pushing him forward.)

Kerensky: The Germans "proclaim friendship" by appealing to your naiveté.

Agitator: Sir, sir, I, ah, they say we must fight so that the peasants may have the land, but I say, we say, of what use is land to me if I'm maimed or killed?"

Kerensky: General, I order you to remove this soldier immediately. Pack him off to his village. Let his fellow villagers know that the

Russian Revolution has no need of cowards. (Messenger enters hands dispatch to General.)

General: Thank you Prime Minister. (Waves dispatch.) Do you know what this is? It's news confirming what I have said all along. While German agents and certain individuals among you have been shooting off their mouths in place of bullets calling for peace and fraternizing with your enemy and you listen like babes in the woods, they have gone behind your back and bombed Stokhad. (Soldiers: Boo!) Are we going to take this deceit lying down? Take up your arms, men! Defend your honor, your country! (Loud cheering.)

Kerensky: Agitators and Bolsheviks will go on undermining your loyalty while they are in service to Germany. Stand with your new government for the sake of Russia. Re–summon the will to fight for the Fatherland. Harsh as it sounds. I hate to say it. I speak of the will to die for your country. If Russia is to survive its army and its people must have a strong will to die for their country. Once that will dissolves we are doomed. Forward to the battle of freedom! I summon you not to feast but to death! We call you to social revolution not to die for others, but to destroy others, to destroy class enemies in the front and the rear! (Blackout. Stepping into spot Dwn R.) My government dissolved all censures of exiles at home and abroad. All could return without fear of arrest including Lenin who repaid us by subversion at every turn. To this day some people think Stalin was good for Russia. It attests to continued ignorance. One dead body in the name of justice is one too many. Some called me weak and inept. I never ordered the cold–blooded shooting of comrades, citizens, or the Tsar's entire family. As Prime Minister I saw to it that those we'd displaced were handled with dignity even the worst offenders. It takes more strength not to give in to revenge. Sadly, the most ignorant of the masses preferred rapine and murder, and followed the Bolshevik counter–revolution. The final scene in the fight between the Provisional Government and the Bolshevik Right and Left took place in the days prior to October 26*th* (November 7.) 1917. General Kornilov's failed coup d'etat set the table for Bolshevik lies and false propaganda sponsored by self–aggrandizing bankers, financiers, and agents–provocateur. Our military was dispirited from a rotten autocracy that got us into an unwanted war ill–equipped and led by inept commanders. The Tsar himself had foolishly taken command of the troops in Mohelif without an ounce of military experience. You see, General Kornolov's supporters had a fall–back plan. They encouraged the Bolshevik *uprising*, even helped it, thinking that afterward they would move in and crush them with the military. The civil and military thinking of these traitors was that the Bolsheviks could never hold onto power and within a month "sound elements" of the Russian people would make short shrift of them. I spoke to the Council of the Republic: *I have incontrovertible evidence of Lenin and his organization's plans for an uprising. Measures are being taken to defend the government.* But the council was torn by discord and differences of opinion, and wasted a whole day in quarrels and disputation. It is a common failure of people to *comprehend* events occurring before them or to perceive the causation and connection of these events. Midnight on the 25*th* of October I had a stormy session with the Left majority in the council on adoption of my resolution to act. I threatened resignation. Dan said I was less informed than they were, that I exaggerated the threat, my staff overreacted, and by tomorrow the Bolsheviki would disband and melt away. You have to understand; these people were skilled in putting off business at hand until *tomorrow*, and never the moment a decision was most needed. Politicians are good at planning for yesterday. Ask them about tomorrow, they'll say call me the day after. They didn't want to act out of fear of *disturbing* the people. In the end the people were disturbed beyond their wildest dreams. At that time, the Red Guard was moving in taking over government buildings. The Council of the Republic in failing to act enabled the Bolsheviks to gain the advantage. Then in comes a Cossack delegation headed by two officers who said they would defend the government only they wanted assurance their blood would not be spilled in vain. I told them I was at the front in July, but took action on my return, ordered arrests of Bolshevik chiefs, and dismissed General Polovzoff of command for lack of decision during that uprising. I signed an agreement with the Cossacks never doubting they would do otherwise. But they did. Soldiers who had sworn oaths reneged when most needed. It's the height of dishonor. My mistake was in not knowing that while I dealt with the Cossacks at hand, the Council of Cossack Troops had decided on a neutral stance in the struggle between the Provisional Government and the Bolsheviks. Meanwhile, the Red Guard seized the central telephone station, the main post office, government buildings, were closing in on the Winter Palace, the Military District Staff Headquarters, and setup headquarters at Smolny Institute. Plans were made to recapture the building. Colonel Polkovnikoff's attitude seemed odd to me. He was too optimistic, too smug, and reassuring that things were under control. The truth is they were not. It became clear his information about troop attitude and staff readiness to take decisive measures against the Bolsheviki were without substance, and, as I surmised later on, played into the hands of the enemy. Frankly, it entered my mind but I quickly rejected it, that some of these people were ignorant or saboteurs. Rovsky then came to me; he was the government's commissar bringing disturbing and contradictory news about the situation. A number of Baltic Fleet Warships had entered the Neva forming battle positions. Mutineers who were moving toward the palace bridge held other key crossings, some as far as Nicholayevsky Bridge. He said *there was little resistance from government troops. The staff of the Petrograd military district watched the developments indifferently without a sign of reaction.* It was shocking to me. Allegiances were scattered. People changed sides at the drop of a rumor. Propaganda funded by Germany was all over the place. Because of deceitful ministers in the autocracy, it was hard to know who was telling the truth. You can believe me or not. That is your choice. Then Savinkoff came to me with a paper to sign. I figured it concerned the defense of Gatchina, but no, the paper stated that Kerensky, Commander–In–Chief, commissions Boris Savinkoff, its bearer, to go to General Headquarters for re–enforcements in defense of Gatchina. He asked me to please sign it and I did. The request was unnecessary. I now understood the situation had reached a turning point. Plainly, Savinkoff was abandoning his post and me. It was senseless to talk about it. *There were damn few reliable people.* I could no longer tell what side anybody was on. Treachery abounded. To save Gatchina would've taken a miracle. The reinforcements I sent for still hadn't come and that made the Cossacks fear treachery from me. They thought I could no longer save them from the anger of the people. I had no news from the front or Petrograd. The old Gatchina palace's endless corridors were gloomy and filled with angry people. Rumors flew about: If the Cossacks gave me up they could all go home. Betrayal was on everyone's mind. The night seemed eternal. Rats deserting a sinking ship! The day before people surrounded me. Now there was no one. Only the silence of the tomb. I burned important papers and then rested. I was awakened by Dybenko's report that a decision had been reached. The sailors and Cossacks want me to surrender to the Bolsheviks. Clearly, General Krasnoff had betrayed us. He allowed sailors in the palace, but claimed they were harmless. He wanted me to go to Petrograd and make an agreement with the Bolsheviks at Smolny all for the sake of saving the country. His nervous manner, lack of eye contact, his odd way of smiling, told me where he stood. I said I'd think on it. I was trapped. Escape seemed impossible with guards everywhere. A palace keeper spoke of a secret underground exit, but we'd have to use it after dark. I, and Lieutenant Vinner decided we'd end our lives with revolvers rather than surrender alive to traitors. Around three PM a soldier ran in pale faced. The Cossacks had bought their freedom and the right to go home for the price of my head. Sailors and Cossacks were about to come for me. Later I learned, it's in the archives, that General Dukhonin received a note from General Krasnoff saying I ordered Commander–In–Chief Kerensky's arrest, but he escaped. General Dukhonin believed that my arrest was ordered because I had planned to make a deal with the Bolsheviks, a falsehood.

Mamushka: Excuse me. Is it true you escaped in one of my dresses?.

Kerensky: Please, Mamushka. It was melodramatic enough. If the military or Bolsheviks had captured me I would've been hung from the nearest rafter.

Mamushka: How did you escape?

Kerensky: You see everyone was preoccupied. Some guards had just arrived, and didn't know the situation. Others had grown weary of duty and were not on the lookout for an escapee like me. (Enter sailor and soldier.)

Sailor: Sir, there is no time to lose.
Soldier: Put on these things: a sailor's coat and hat.
Sailor: And these automobile goggles.
Kerensky: No, no. The coat is short. The hat is too small.
Sailor: Don't move your head. It'll stay on. I'll go on ahead. (Exits.)
Soldier: Sir, time is short. It's the best we could do. Hurry. The Bolsheviks are already entering the front of the building.
Kerensky: (To audience.) The hat and the goggles struck me as an obvious absurdity. Well, the noose was tightening around my neck and there was no time to form an intelligent plan. Sometimes under pressure the corniest idea sudden, swift, and unexpected wins the day. There was no time to think. The disguise was outlandish, but beggars can't be choosy.
Soldier: A get away car is waiting at the palace gate. Is there a back way out?
Kerensky: Yes. (To audience.) We exited through the secret door in my bedroom descended a narrow stairway to where there was a long empty corridor that seemed eternal. Suddenly two sailors step out from behind a pillar directly in my path. I held my breath.
Sailor 1: Have you a light, comrade? Spacebo. (They go.)
Kerensky–Sailor–Soldier: More stairs. Yes. It is the last of them and then the exit, the only one. It's guarded. Keep walking. One mistake, a false step, and we're dead. (Salutes all around. Outside under the arch.)
Kerensky: No one is following us. Good Lord! It's incredible. Strange. Maybe they've seen so many odd things lately one more doesn't matter; goggles, a short sailor coat and a hat that keeps slipping off.
Sailor: Up ahead. The outer gate.
Kerensky: No automobile. No one. Have we been betrayed?
Soldier: Walk slowly a little further on. Slowly. There's a mix–up. We go back.
Kerensky: My God! That begs the question.
(An exchange of good morning passes between them and a door guard.)
Kerensky: Back in the soup. A miracle.

Sailor: Head toward the guardroom. (Distant rush of noise.) Dybenko's sailors, and Krasnoffs Cossacks are coming upstairs to get you.
Kerensky: Who is that coming toward us?
Sailor: The fellow who told us about the car.
Soldier: (Casual not stopping.) Mistake. Automobile at Egyptian gate town exit.
Sailor: Quickly. Back again under the arch.
Kerensky: This gets crazier by the second and more dangerous.
(A guard approaches them. Suddenly, an officer emerges from the shadows in bandages, scars on his face, the look of battle fatigue. He steps in front of the guard, faints; Kerensky and others slip out the door.)
Sailor: A cab. Let's take it. (They jump in a cab.)
Kerensky: Up ahead. The Egyptian gates.
Sailor: And our car. The chauffeur's an aviator.
Kerensky: I wish he'd brought a plane.
Chauffeur: We'll take the chausée to Luga. On the seat grenades in case we need them.
(Back at the palace.)
Dybenko: No Kerensky. He's not in his office or his bedroom.
Kerenky's Aide: What? Impossible. O, there's that back door in his bedroom. He is headed for the Egyptian Gates. His personal car is here. I have the key. Let's get that scoundrel.
(In the get–away car.)
Sailor: A car is following us. Step on it.
Kerensky: They've pulled off the road.
Sailor: Around the next turn is a wooded area with a peasant house. The people are plain honest folks. Nobody is along the chausée in either direction.
Kerensky: (To audience.) We disappear into the woods while our car speeds ahead as a diversion, the horn–sounding goodbye in the distance. Now the Bolsheviks were in power and held on. With the fall of Gatchina the story closed on the Provisional Government and me.

Tauride Palace

Lenin: (Moves DC into spot light.) Word reached us in the early morning hours quietly without fanfare or exultation. The people had triumphed. The ease with which we overthrew the coalition government revealed its impotence, and the degree of that impotence amazed even the well informed. The Tsar seemed hardly aware that it was a question of his ineptitude, that of his class, and the social structure. Now it was time to tend to *necessary business*.

Scene 3

Fanya: (Rising angrily.) I'm a radical Left Socialist–Revolutionary, so they say. Let them. *Govoryat shto kur doyat.* They also say you can milk chickens. Tfu. On August 30, 1918 I shot Lenin. He subverted the original intention of the revolution with guns and false promises further splitting socialist revolutionaries. The revolution wasn't about trading one dictator for another. Lenin was a grand speechmaker, but his words belied his actions.
Lenin: Everyone sees according to his or her own light. At some point theory must be put into practice with allowances for error.
Fanya: The Central Committee desiring to move forward talked of compromise between Bolsheviks and Mensheviks, a coalition.
Lenin: No. I disagree. No coalition. Compromise on little things, but on big ones be resolute. Kill if need be. What shall history say of us, of our revolution, as it sifts the records under a mountain of dead dogs in search of truth? Examining us under a microscope—each word, journal, article, photo, turning each leaf, each possibility, running down every lead, every voice—and why, comrade, why, to get at the truth, which will never be known.
Trotsky: Lenin, believing the time was ripe for an uprising based on the rise of anti–government feeling spearheaded a strike for power that would coincide with the next all–Russian Congress of Soviets. The other socialist parties opposed his plan. I was dubious myself.

Fanya: We thought it premature, would backfire, and destroy what gains had been made at the time. The people liked the idea of land distribution but not Bolshevik communism. The Duma (Council) was set for open elections, which Lenin suspended at gunpoint.

Lenin: Elections have never decided a major political change.

Fanya: Civil war was a result of your coup.

Lenin: Vote counts take time in which events and opportunities pass you by.

Fanya: Opportunity for you to take control of government. The people revolted against tsarism, demanded peace, land, and bread. The civil war was the 3rd revolution against you; not as claimed instigated and funded by the West fearful of spreading socialism. You, *Heir Lenin*, brought on three years of unspeakable bloodshed. Millions died in combat or from hunger, cold, and disease. (Mimicking.) *Well, you can't make an omelet without breaking an egg*. Tfu! It was the start of War Communism, whipping the people to your way of thinking. After the fighting we suffered a greater enemy, famine, Asian in magnitude. So Russia thanks you. The millions who died thank you. But you never fooled me. Class warfare was at the heart of your plan all along because you knew the old way would not go gently. You were out to spread civil discord across Europe and the world. To you civil war meant conflict between you, Oberhaupt (chief.),—Yah!—Oberbefehlshaber (commander–in–chief) of the new proletarian army, versus everybody else: the nobility, the dreaded Bourgeoisie—in a class war of which the military conflict was only one dimension. You're like a troubadour with a guitar singing socialist hymns from on high while the people kill each other. In a social and political sense our Civil War never ended. It went underground. The new leaders ought to take note of that and be wary and always perform their sworn duty on behalf of the people.

Kerensky: Explain that Duma business?

Fanya: He had Bull–shevik goon squads in the street intimidating, and killing rivals. (Gallery Voices Booo!) When it came to a Duma vote by assembly representatives of various nationwide constituencies on which party should govern, Lenin shut off the electricity, closed the Duma, barred the gates, and posted armed guards to keep voters out.

Kerensky: Why?

Fanya: Because Lenin was a traitor to the revolution! Because in a free and fair election *he would've lost.* So I dipped the bullets in strychnine in case they missed.

Kerensky: Why didn't the poison kill him?

Fanya: Why in deed. (Sarcastic.) The great Lenin died like his nobleman father from cerebral hemorrhage. More Bull–shevik manure designed to protect their image. Lenin's nose wasn't always between the pages of Marx and Engels.

Kerensky: Oh?

Fanya: No, sir. Let us say it was in the horse latitudes between the labia majora and the labia minora. On arrival in Pete, what an ovation! Thousands cheered. *Workers of the world unite!* He did lots of uniting, and dismounting. *You have nothing to lose but your chains and some your virginity.* With hearts glowing the fools sang the Marseilles, and walked straight into the loving arms of Frankenstalin totalitarian communism. Better the devil you know than the one you don't know.

Kerensky: You see what I had to contend with?—A bag of mixed nuts: the nobility, the monarchists, and the officers class on one side, socialist communists on the other and in between bitterness so deep it drove families apart. It got so that being Russian or having common blood meant nothing. Each side saw the other as devils incarnate. We had the <u>outward</u> look of control and power in domestic and foreign affairs, but <u>inwardly</u> we were three sheets to the wind. Everyone had ideas, and plans on how to run things, but not how to implement them. While we ran the bureaucracy the streets were in the hands of the Petrograd Soviets who led the workers and soldiers. We needed funds to build up our fighting forces and to supply them properly. The Root commission representing our Western allies came to Russia, saw what was happening, and said in effect do not pull out of the war, *no fight, no funds.* I initiated a military buildup, launched an offensive on the Galician front,—A mistake.—The morale and the deterioration of the military had already gone too far. The army had to tuck tail and retreat yet again. It was horrible to see that the will and spirit had gone out of our fighting men. I attribute it to all the fractious groups constantly at each other's throats pulling every which way but together. Then of course there were the Bolsheviks carrying on serpentine propaganda more on their behalf than for the welfare of Russia. Of all the groups they were the most extreme and most violent toward everyone else. They would do whatever it took to bring us down, from instilling doubts and fears to calling us the enemy. It was an indescribable time. The Bolsheviks cried *No Confidence* and *No Trust* in us when it was they who lacked those qualities. Later on an American described it fairly well: *Responsibility without power confronted power without responsibility.*

General Deniken: (Rising.) We patriotic officers felt ourselves humiliated by the destruction of the Russian army, sabotaged by Bolshevik propaganda and their betrayal of commitments to our allies. Slice it how you will. To our way of thinking, Lenin plain and simple was the war agent of the Kaiser, a traitor to all Russia. The man harbored deep-seated resentments mixed with earnest high-minded dreams and desires. Lenin was always ten feet ahead of himself. His body was in this world, but his mind in another. I wanted to stop the fratricidal war that the Bolsheviks let loose. Our position was anti-German attempting to reverse Lenin's success in transforming a war between nations into a war between classes. Civil War started October 1917 when the Bolsheviks toppled the Provisional Government and then suppressed all rival political parties at gunpoint. Understand me, it was a time of great anxiety.

Kerensky: One can say with certainty that Civil War ended on April 23, 1921.

General Deniken: Against your political adversaries, yes, but it was far from over beyond your nose. In the country at large war had just started. Allow me to reiterate that *in a social and political sense the Russian Civil War never ended.*

Kerensky: Thank you. Frederick Engels owned a factory. He had his employees work overtime to increase production in order to raise revenue to support Karl Marx who in 1848 wrote The Communist Manifesto, 24 pages about communal sharing that became the bible for another excuse to kill millions of people. Had Lenin not died from a stroke–

Fanya: Bah! You misguided historians, keepers of the fraudulent flame. Bah! He had been taking strychnine for years—the only known cure for a disease he'd contracted around 1903. Of course the bullets didn't help his disposition. One was inoperable and remained lodged in his neck.

Trotsky: Starting in 1921 Lenin had the first of three strokes, which ended his life in 1924. The official explanation said *degenerative brain disease*. The one with a degenerative brain disease was Stalin. When Ilych died I was off on Party business. Stalin cabled me saying Lenin's funeral was on Sunday; that morning I took an early train to Moscow to find it had taken place Saturday.

Fanya: You Bull–shevik artist. Why didn't you phone a colleague to verify, and to commiserate? You merely accepted the word of a man you distrusted. Bah!

Trotsky: I admit the mistake.

Fanya: It speaks to a poor relationship with your colleagues. Where was your head, comrade, up your ass?

Stalin: Ha, ha, ha. (Shakes foot at Trotsky.)

Trotsky: Your seminary fathers were right in expelling you. Your vocabulary is in your feet. Why did you burn Lenin's intestines?

Stalin: Three guesses.

Trotsky: Lenin mentioned poison to you. (Nods yes.) But direct action is not your cup of tea. (Nods no.) You'd get the doctor to do the job and then have the poor man killed on some trumped up accusation: yanked from bed in the middle of the night, befuddled, confused, and anything he would say in his defense would be seen as the ravings of a lunatic. (Nods yes.) Zinoviev was right. Man to man in open debate you're a push over, but not under cover of night assisted by the relentless KGB perhaps a callow youth incapable of realizing that his actions would mark him for death, too.

Stalin: The first obligation of a revolutionary is to live. Lenin had everything, and then,—Bang! Nothing. Dead and gone at the height of his dreams. Very strange, yes? Ha, ha.

Trotsky: Kemenev told me, "I wouldn't put anything past Stalin." He and Zinoviev told me they had each filed secret letters stating that if anything happened to them it would be your doing. They advised me to do the same. Stalin knows the truth about Lenin's death. Well, what is the truth?

Stalin: For me to know, you to find out.

Trotsky: You burned his intestines.

Stalin: I kept the upper torso for public viewing. After Lenin died you had your moment and let it go.

Trotsky: Yes. I declined high office in the name of harmony, for the sake of cohesion rather than disaffection.

Stalin: For the sake of disaffection rather than cohesion that was *dumb!*

Trotsky: The hunger, broken bone, and the horror of spilled blood does it haunt you so many lives unjustly shortened?

Stalin: Oblamovs, *victims* of their own *gluttony*. While you were *talk, talk, always talking* I, so–so, the gray blur took the bull by the horns. I turned the peasants, kulaks, and villages upside down. Like it or not I moved their dead asses to collectives lock, stock, and barrel in this life not the next. The people had become lethargic canon fodder for the rich; the backbone, the jackasses of society: abused, and condemned to ignorance to satisfy the elite. The irony of it is that the oppressed support their oppressors, sacrifice their lives based on subtle lies couched in the name of duty, God, and country. Were I to say, *Comrade, give me your money and I promise to kick your ass every day of your life,* you would say, *Comrade Stalin, go to the devil!*

Trotsky: That is what governments do.

Stalin: They take your money like a thankless whore, fuck you without a kiss, and kick your ass in the bargain. Well, I reversed it.

Trotsky: To the detriment of the cause.

Stalin: The cause, Lenin's pie in the sky falderal. You can't talk to people who believe in fairy tales, who even to this day think everybody can succeed. How? By the unmentionable: usury. You and the others could weave a good story, but your feet were never on the ground. There is no escaping the glumness of existence so I livened things up, kicked ass. Future pundits will make educated guesses about me, our time, but say this, say it clearly, that what Stalin did in Russia was a major transforming world event equal to Jesus Christ.

Trotsky: For a moment we were on the doorstep of utopia, an arm's reach from a world federation, one people indivisible empathic with reverence for all life.
Stalin: Still with the poetry. I discovered reality in the seminary: you can trust no one least of all the most pious. I tasted duplicitous classmates and petty priests: All of them clinging to resentments and grudges based on self-interest. So, I beat life to the punch. Stir the horseshit and never look back. It's laughable. We thought ourselves invincible.
Trotsky: It's not given to youth to think otherwise. Now it's finished, up in smoke. What will history say of us? Born Leon Davidovich Bronstein on a farm on the steppes of the Ukraine, a disenfranchised Jew who dreamed on a world scale and tripped up.
Stalin: Because I came up from behind and tied your shoelaces. You got soft, and lost the killer instinct. Not me. I got tougher and tougher. Life belongs to the stronger, the one that grabs it by the scruff of the neck, shakes the shit out of it, and never blinks. (Kicks a foot out. Lights out; up on:)
Kerensky: Let us look at the Bolshevik legacy—the worst degradation of a civilized people in history. For starters, the concessions at Brest-Litovsk.
Trotsky: I was against signing that treaty, but it bought us time.
Kerensky: And you got lucky. Germany lost the war.
Trotsky: Yes. Luck was with us when Lenin survived assassination, laughed it off, but it took something out of the old man. Be that as it may, what followed post Lenin exceeded our initial intentions. It was in a word a catastrophe. What I feel rises out of love, and consternation that such madness happened. It tells me that men are certifiable deceivers, outwardly civilized, and inwardly bestial.
Kerensky: Lenin was no guarantee that what followed would've been avoided.
Trotsky: That we shall never know. Certainly, he was well aware of historical patterns in revolutions and cautioned against devisiveness, and Jacobism.
Kerensky: Every revolution eats its children.

Trotsky: I attribute our failure to lack of faith and trust in each other, which resulted in the inevitable classical pattern, vis–à–vis, the French Revolution.
Kerensky: France had Robspirre and Marat–sad, Russia had Lenin and Stalin, but no Charlotte Corday. Why is that?
Stalin: Steel doors and an armored car. Ha, ha.
Fanya: What am I, chopped liver? I should've machine gunned all you bastards.
Trotsky: From the outset we were determined to break the people's infantile devotion to God and the Tsar, and introduce collectivization. I asked Lenin, what is our chance of success? He was fond of quoting Napoleon: "On s'engage et puis, on voit,"—You commit then you see.
Stalin: See? See my ass! What none of you saw was me, *the goddamn gray blur!*
Trotsky: I clung to the hope that differences in ideology would ultimately give way to the Party above all else. I held the naïve and somewhat romantic notion that feelings of camaraderie developed over years of common struggle, of shared hardships, and dreams would bind us as brothers.
Lenin: (Rising suddenly.) I wanted justice for all not just a chosen few.
Kerensky: So you gave us Frankenstalin.
Lenin: A parent cannot be held responsible for everything a child does. Stalin is a product of predatory capitalism and feudal autocracy. Had Tsarism been fair to the people there would've been no Stalin or Lenin. I had to undo centuries of mental damage by legislating conduct with an eye to dropping it once the people accepted the new way: collectivization and rule from below. By Jove the question before us is no mystery. It's the old Platonic problem: what is the best way to live? Change rarely occurs without resistance. Not even the *great so–called American* democracy was born from the head of Zeus full blown. It grew and changed into a plutocracy, a country run by the wealthy. A democracy needs socialism. Why expect our socialist–communism to be perfect from start? In a democracy the people have the right to vote. When they don't, get lazy or indifferent, then capitalists, men with money move in and buy what suits them solely to turn a

profit. This is predatory capitalism where all things are chattel. The slave trade exemplifies turning human rights into commodity. Under socialism–communism the end goal is Jeffersonian democracy moving away from plutocracy to a mix of democracy and socialism. It's happening in America with the rise of unions, which are the *great fear of plutocrats*. Everybody. Repeat after me, *unions are the great fear of plutocrats.* Louder. Again. Tre bon.

Kerensky: How do you account for Stalin? (Pause.) Anybody?

Trotsky: After Lenin's first stroke in 1922 there began a struggle for power among Lenin's cadre. They were too blindsided by vehement opinions, hair splitting, and petty jealousies to see that General Secretary Stalin had his claws in every department giving key jobs to Georgian cronies like Yezhov who headed the secret police, and others hungry for work to earn money to buy a piece of bread to keep from starving to death. Naturally, they were beholden to him. Remember, we'd been through a World War and a Civil War. Jobs were at a premium. People had no money, no food, and couldn't pay their bills. Stalin doled out jobs. How could one not feel obligated? This was all done discreetly. In time he built an organization that couldn't operate without him. All the while in the General Assembly and the Politburo he watched and waited, observed and made mental notes on everyone and everything. He gave the appearance of a good listener without an opinion. When it came time to vote on business he invariably voted with the majority. So naturally when Lenin denounced him, and he offered to resign it was only natural the politburo members wouldn't hear of it. One way or another he had them all in his pocket.

Kerensky: Lenin had a blueprint. L'etat e mois—I am the state.

Lenin: It was necessary to make a start.

Kerensky: But the finish exceded the worst evils of the monarchy at its height. The record shows that in 1907 you were brought before a tribunal of peers–

Lenin: For "Impermissible language" towards the Mensheviks of the Central Committee. It came to nothing. However, allow me to take moment to explain it to you. The Menshviks claimed I *exceeded the parameters of acceptable conduct in polemical discussion,* a serious breech of etiquette. If a party splits there are no polemical limits. A split implies cessation of the existence of a party. The limits of a struggle based on a split are not party limits, but general political or civil limits established by Criminal Law, nothing more. All party members owe disciplined obedience to their party. But do you understand? The party split! So I attacked the Mensheviks for selling workers' votes to the Cadets in a Petersburg Election that was unethical. There were more fraternal ways to unite opposition to the Tsar than selling votes. My words were meant to bring out the worst suspicions about the Mensheviks to evoke hatred, aversion and contempt for them for committing such deeds . . . not to convince or correct a mistake, but to break up the Menshevik ranks . . . to destroy this organization. I caused that section of the proletariat which trusts the Mensheviks to waver. I was out to carry confusion into the ranks of the proletariat. Now do I believe such calculations are impermissible? Certainly, but with the following proviso: Impermissible among members of a united party. A split means the rupture of organizational ties, the shifting of the struggle of ideas from correcting and persuading comrades to that of destroying their organization, to inciting the masses of workers and peoples generally against the seceded organization. It is wrong to write about party comrades in a way that spreads among the working masses hatred, aversion, contempt for those who hold different opinions. We must not fall into the trap of Jacobism.

Kerensky: You carried confusion into the ranks of the Petersburg proletariat.

Lenin: Yes. Into the ranks which had followed the Mensheviks who seceded. When a split has taken place it is one's duty to wrest the masses from the leadership of the seceded section. I shall always act in that way whenever a split occurs. Against such political enemies I shall always conduct a fight of extermination. As to restraints by criminal law, these would vanish when one's party became the government and made the law.

Kerensky: Did you consider back then what would happen with this blueprint of yours when taken by men of lesser ingrained humaneness, and concern for the long–term effect on the understanding of the masses, or when it is adopted by the leaders of other communist parties, lacking the counter balancing human tradition of the old Russian revolutionary intelligentsia?

Lenin: I never expected to die. The greater fight is always biology.
Kerensky: All the good, earnest fighters went down for your *cause* to an ignominious grave. Three years of civil war, a failed New Economic Policy (Collectivization), a supposed cornerstone of communism, and the wretched Stalin—that inhuman, remorseless gutter rat of the revolution, your Frankenstein, a scumbag of bile and spleen gone amok. It speaks volumes.
Lenin: You'll get no argument on that.
Kerensky: So many people butchered and slaughtered one another in your name; others cut off from life, isolated in the frozen tundra of Siberia to die from exposure, or reduced through systematic torture to idiots and suicide. Still others pretended to escape and in fleeing prayed the guard's bullet would be swift and merciful. The luckier ones survived, brushing with death daily, clinging to life by a slender thread of hope: millions dislocated because of your sublimated revenge for the hanging of your brother.
Lenin: (Erupting.) Shut that filthy bourgeois mouth! You dare speak of my brother who is above reproach? Who among you is so brave and loyal a son that you'd willingly stick your neck in a noose for your country? At 18 years of age Sasha was such a man, a boy with the heart of an innocent. And you dare to utter his name? A man who when it came to crunch time deserted Russia. Even now with one foot in the Pearly Gates you remain a simpleton. My brother Sasha was . . . goddamn you. (Chokes.) People like you are the real terrorists, the destroyers of individuality and initiative. Attempting to kill the Tsar was against Sasha's inborn sense of honor, but like Vera Figner and others he had no choice. He refused to recant. The monarchy that should've apologized, but instead it murdered its best son. Like Socrates in a dissembling world Sasha had the guts of his convictions and refused to live a lie.
Kerensky: The argument is what you and Trotsky did to your country.
Lenin: I died too early.
Trotsky: *We build statues out of snow and weep to see them melt.*
Kerensky: Trotsky you must've wondered at some point where is the money coming from to pay the tab for the *sealed train*,

the food, lodging, paper and ink, printing machines, fliers and pamphlets, etcetera, etcetera?

Trotsky: Contributions from wealthy sympathizers. Friends provided rooms in their homes. We subsisted on basics. Granted that on the surface some of what you suggest is true, but you well know at bottom Lenin was a Russian patriot.

Lenin: Leon, one can't argue against opinion.

Trotsky: Around 1925 the Politburo offered me the Chairmanship. I refused it. I saw the way things were going, the misery and death, and it saddened me. Little by little our ideals were shunted aside. More and more we were becoming the tyranny we had overthrown.

Kerensky: So you left it to comrade Stalin–

Trotsky: Who knew then what a monster we had among us? I believed we all held some sense of camaraderie and loyalty to each other based on the years we'd shared together. I was grievously mistaken, sufficiently naïve to think that friends don't lie to each other.

Kerensky: On the contrary, they do. That's why they are friends.

Trotsky: Where Lenin's old guard had traveled the world, were fluent in languages, he was a slacker, booted out of seminary school, and educated in the street. It was unimaginable that such brutishness could exist in our coterie of cynical intellectuals. By the time Lenin realized Stalin's true character he was too sick to act. Still, he warned us from his dying bed. Strangely enough we didn't fully grasp his meaning. *Stalin will bring disgrace to the Party.* The words were plain enough, but in an abstract sense. Then, too, the Party was beset by factional infighting. While various elements jockeyed for power, Stalin kept his position on issues and his proclivities for evil well hidden until he was in a position to let them loose. It was as if one day we all woke up to find there was a crocodile in the room. No one suspected. I dare say, even Stalin himself didn't know the extent of his vengeful mind. His appetite for evil grew on the thing it fed, turning him into a glutton for blood and death. There is an Old Russian proverb: When you meet a man you judge him by his clothes; when you leave, you judge him by his heart. With Stalin we missed the boat on both counts. By the time we woke up to the truth it was too late to act. In hindsight everything is always clearer. *A man can smile and yet be a villain.* It's a wonder that civilization has progressed as far as it has. We at least know enough to band together. Toward the end Stalin kept Lenin isolated saying it was for Lenin's own good. I say it was for Stalin's good. My surmise is that Lenin succumbed from poison. As a comrade later said, I wouldn't put anything past Stalin. Krupskaya got suspicious and angry about the isolation of her husband. Stalin got nasty, Lenin found out. That's when he wrote the note. Our failure was loss of original intention. We lost our vision and sense of direction. What became essential was survival by whatever means even tyranny. Early on Lenin said half jokingly, *if Stalin gets in a position of power he will serve up some peppery dishes.* We laughed. We were young, felt the glow of youth and the strength in our muscles. Such a possibility of Stalin amounting to anything was remote, ridiculous, and unimaginable. The man was a low life, couldn't write, wasn't bi–lingual, had poor oratory skills, and his Russian speech retained a vulgar Georgian accent offensive to the ear.

Nadya: Stalin had Ilych isolated. I insisted on seeing my husband. Still he refused me. Normally, I'm a quiet woman not given to shouting and screaming or profanity, but when he started swearing and cursing! Regrettably my temper flared. *Stalin, you overstep yourself. You have the manners of a mongrel.* He started to speak, but I cut him short. *Comrade, I wasn't born yesterday. Your impudence is intolerable. Do not presume to tell me about party politics, which I helped shape.* Ilych found out and wrote a memo to the Central Committee denouncing Stalin as *an ill–mannered brute who in time would bring discredit to the party, and should be banished from the organization.*

Trotsky: First off, Stalin was made Secretary General of the Party years before Lenin's death. Stalin was in charge of administrative duties, personnel, setting the day's agenda for committee meetings that would deliberate the business before them including general opinions held for and against each proposal. He was in charge of hiring personnel to run the various administrative departments and overseeing all of the details that many of the inner circle of top functionaries disdained feeling it was beneath them. Nothing was beneath Stalin. He embraced every piece of government business including the police department. In addition to a personnel record he built private dossiers like an impeccable paranoid that included the most intrusive details of someone's character that I dare say bordered voyeurism. He kept extensive notes on everyone: how they voted, their opinion on political questions, their associates, their predilections in food and sex. It was all done with an eye to the future. From the beginning of his early criminal days in Georgia between 1900 and 1912, the year he was admitted into the Party, when he was a police informer his twisted mind saw life like his fellow Georgian mountaineers who carry grudges and never forgive a slight. He trained himself to wait patiently for the day of revenge. Stalin had no interest in the cultural things of life like music, art, and philosophy. He had little interest in women. In fact, I don't think his second wife was a suicide. They had many arguments after she learned what sort of man she had married: his insensitivity toward others, the pain he inflicted on people and their families. That last night they argued, he lost control, shot her, made it look like suicide, and then played the distraught and bereaved party the way he did when he had Kirov assassinated. You understand me? The man could shake your hand, stab you in the back, and you'd die thinking it was someone else. As for women? Revenge was his orgasm. Do you understand what I am saying?

Stalin: To deceive the deceiver is twice the joy.

Trotsky: To point up how devious Stalin was as a politician, he was an anti–Semite yet Bukharin, Zinoviev and Kamenev all Jews sided with him and not me for Party Chairman. Later on, Bukharin joined forces with me, but by then it was already too late.

Kerensky: You were smarter than all of them, perhaps too smart, and in some ways arguably superior to Lenin.

Trotsky: In life one has to watch where he puts his feet. They lived to regret it.

Stalin: Doctrinal authority is unassailable whatever the cost. The Party elite interprets, decides policy at any given time, and their decisions must be absolute. It's the price of living in society. Nothing rivals the anticipation of that sweet time when the knife enters and is slowly twisted while you're home having a good night's sleep. Revenge is best served cold.

Mamushka: (Gaveling.) Gorbatogo mogila ispravit. Only the grave cures the hunchback. (Lights out.)

ACT 7

Dacha Nights

Scene 1

Place: *Stalin's dacha outside Moscow.*
Time: 1931–1933.

Coachie: Russia of 1917 was still feudal, eighty percent of the people were illiterate. Who would've believed that 45 years later a Russian would be first to walk in space? How much further we might've come had the flower of our youth not been—Well, Stalin's own daughter defected. (Enter Svetlana.) I'd known her as a child, an adorable ray of sunshine. Ride, my dear?
Svetlana: Yes, thank you, Uncle Sergei!
Coachie: Dah. My coach is yours. Shh. Penance. It's a living. Where to?
Svetlana: After all you've done how could you? Why a cabbie?
Coachie: I like telling people where to get off. Ha. You like my joke? It's true though. Svetka, tell me something I could never understand. How could you turn your back on family and country?
Svetlana: It was the most difficult decision of my life, and yet so simple once I decided to go. My father whom I dearly loved as a child, but in growing up things no longer looked the same, made the decision for me. What he had done, what he was doing, and his atheism became unbearable for me. My first husband was an educated man, a scientist; but father never liked him because he was smart and a Jew. In time I had to divorce him.
Coachie: That was disagreeable business, but one did not contradict Stalin. Whom you married was a matter of indifference to me except that you married for love.

Svetlana: Then there was the critical matter of religion. I believe in God and father was an atheist. He thought religion was ludicrous, a hoax put over on the people. He would poke fun at me, call me ignorant, and tell me to grow up. In time it became intolerable. I did not want to spend my life like so many of my countrymen sneaking around corners to pray to God always fearful of that immanent footfall of the secret police. As you know very well religion to Russians is like bread, the staff of life. Some time after my divorce I remarried an Indian man. We honeymooned in India and that was when I made up my mind never to return to Russia. It was a heart breaking decision, but I had to do it. Much of it linked to what happened to my mother. As a child I didn't understand any of these things. To me father was everything. He doted on me until I began to think for myself. He became more and more single minded on every subject from religion to politics. I found myself suffocating in his clutches. In the end I no longer trusted his word because of too many contradictions. I refused to accept a way of life that stifles the human spirit. Of course, I miss my country, my friends, my family, and you. But my heart and soul cried out for God and justice. As I grew older the puzzling circumstances surrounding mother's death came together and pointed to father.

Coachie: Stalin was extremely difficult to figure out. Like Vodka, he was odorless. You never knew where you stood with him. He was suspicious of everything. Maybe he liked me because of my relative innocence, which he would push to the point where you had to decide whether it was your life or somebody else's. Then, too, I never offered him advice, never contradicted him, and when I spoke I always told him things he liked to hear. He judged loyalty by how far you were willing to go. Kaganovich, a member of the Politburo, formerly a leather worker and tough administrator from our Georgia days, was my mentor, but in time I saw his real character. Stalin required blood as proof of loyalty to him. Kaganovich gave up his own brother. This meant Stalin had you in his pocket. Life more often presents us with a choice of more evils rather than goods. The trick is survival.

Svetlana: At what price?

Coachie: That is for each man to decide. We men learn fast to hide one thing in the heart while speaking another. I made my biggest decision during my first invitation to your father's nightly elitist soirees at his country dacha.
Svetlana: Their dirty hands in every phase of government.
Coachie: Perhaps I mention this to pacify guilt. As a callow youth I was in the spirit of collectives, of honest work, of Russia rising up, of showing the world what it was made of, and I swallowed the Party Doctrine hook, line and sinker. In my enthusiasm I thought your father was our genius leader. I laugh now that I have seen the elephant and heard the owl. But back then I truly believed your father was Russia's savior. In for a penny, in for a pound. I am not proud of the things I have done yet had I not asserted myself we'd have never met and I would be dead long ago.
Svetlana: My first husband used to quote a Jewish proverb that says *if a man is destined to drown he will drown even in a spoonful of water.*
Coachie: Da.
Svetlana: I used to love sitting on your lap at the movies. You still smell of tobacco and spearmint. On those occasions I used to get upset when the movie finished and I was packed off to bed. I'd fall asleep wondering about the distant noises, shouts, and the music.
Coachie: My first invitation to your father's inner circle was a thrilling moment. For the first time I met informally Beria, Molotov, Voroshilov, and others. But as the night wore on I found I had no escape. The usual routine and fair–
Svetlana: I remember the movies, American westerns.
Coachie: Followed by a late supper and heavy drinking.
Svetlana: Way beyond my bedtime.
Coachie: And mine. Your father favored cowboy movies dealing in revenge, something he understood intuitively. The movies were in English, which nobody understood, not even the projectionist who would translate. He described what we saw and not what was said. "The Indians are chasing the Americans." Da! Good! "The Americans are chasing the Indians." Boo! Nyet. Beria had a good sense of humor, anticipating what the projectionist would

say, and we'd laugh. *What's he doing now? Is he getting off his horse or on it? Now he rides away. O, I missed that. Look. Stalin is sitting in his chair.* Every night was a repeat of the night before: movie to dining room everyone sitting in their regular seats talking, taking notes on the Boss' wishes, and repeating the same old stories that had proven to be acceptable, and therefore, safe to indulge in.

Svetlana: Father had a keen ear for hypocrisy.

Coachie: He would read in between the lines more than was intended often driven by mercurial moods.

Svetlana: I could never tell him a fib. He'd look at me and then the truth would be all over my face.

Coachie: Truth and lies were all the same to him. To be near him was to walk a fine line between here and the hereafter.

Svetlana: His desolation and empty insides did not let him see that people could be warm and sincere.

Coachie: Such emotions were a luxury he couldn't afford.

Svetlana: In old age father was the victim of his own machinations embodied in the monster Beria.

Coachie: At those late supper the usual people were present, the usual talk, the usual sharp asides, the same old jokes and stories. Those 'ordeals', as I came to know them, went on forever, and were deadly for me because I had to report to work early the next day.

Svetlana: Why didn't you make your apologies—Well, I think I know.

Coachie: Ha, ha. You'd have to be on your deathbed, my dear, and even then it might be acceptable protocol. Ha, ha.

Svetlana: What?

Coachie: If you were at death's door Stalin would pull you through. Even a legitimate excuse could prove ruinous. Funny yet not funny. As insulated and guarded at your father was he still had a great fear of being poisoned. Beria, too, feared it.

Svetlana: For good reason. Out of what one does comes fear of being done to.

Coachie: They both had ways of protecting themselves. Your father would wait for others to drink or eat before indulging himself. As I say, it was my first invitation, the hour was well after midnight, and we'd imbibed plenty. It was unavoidable. Stalin watched you like a hawk. To him drinking loosened the tongue, revealed the real man. Let's face it men are not women. Men unlike woman are not openly affectionate, but hold back, and pugnacious by nature. Stalin plied you with drinks, relaxed your defenses, and that was how he got the goods on you. Then, of course, your goose was cooked. So everyone was in his regular seat talking, joking, and drinking heavily when Stalin himself made an insightful slip of the tongue: a damning self–description which over the years rang truer and truer like a hammer hitting an anvil.

Scene 2

Place: Combined living and dining room Stalin's dacha; motion picture setup.)

Projectionist: The hero rides his horse.
Beria: Thank you for that news. I thought it was a camel.
Projectionist: He gets off his horse.
Beria: Better than his horse gets off him. (Laughter.) Draws his gun.
Projectionist: He draws his gun.
Beria: O, a gun. I thought it was licorice. What is he doing now?
Projectionist: He climbs up on his horse.
Beria: Thanks for that clarification. The End!
Projectionist: The end. To be continued. Chapter 14 tomorrow. (Lights up.)
Stalin: American movies make me hungry. (Heads for the dining room.) Beria!
Beria: I'm coming as fast as I can.
Stalin: Sneaking drinks while imperialist America is stealing the West.
Beria: (Entering.) I was complimenting the projectionist for his translation skill. Those Indians can ride . . . and bareback! I have trouble sitting in my chair.
Stalin: What else's new?
Beria: Actually I made a suggestion to the projectionist.

Kaganovich: He's the third one this month. Soon we'll have to go to Siberia to watch movies.
Beria: I asked him to show the movie tomorrow night–
Molotov: Again?
Voroshylov: That will be the ninth time.
Beria: He is going to show the movie in reverse so all the Indians end up back on their land hunting buffalo and scalping American capitalists.
All: O! Splendid! Da, da! Ha, ha! Good!
Molotov: A toast to the Americanski Indians.
All: Nasdrovia! (They drink.)
Voroshylov: To scalping.
All: Nasdrovia!
Molotov: Scalping is a good deterrent.
Beria: The best part of the movie.
Voroshylov: Who started scalping first, the Indians or Americans?
Stalin: Lavrenty. Now reincarnated as Beria. A toast to Beria.
All: Nasdrovia.
Beria: To the Boss's dacha the cathedral of spiritual indulgence.
All: Nasdrovia!
Stalin: Straighten out your collar, Beria. I refuse to drink with a man whose collar is twisted. Yours is twisted like your mind.
Beria: My mind is not twiss–twisted.
Stalin: That's bad news. It's a job requirement.
Beria: Matryona Petrovna! Food! Not twisted, but tortuous.
Stalin: A toast to comrade Beria's tortuous mind.
Everybody: Nasdrovia!
Stalin: A toast to our new comrade from Georgia. Where the hell is he?
Beria: He hasn't been here long enough to disappear.
Stalin: Sergeiyevich! Where are you, under the table already?
Beria: Sleeping in the toilet. Maybe he fell in.
Stalin: Sergeiyevich!! (HE enters tightening his belt.) There you are. Come. Open this bottle. Fill your glass. (HE complies.) Drink. Good, yes? (HE drinks, nods shyly, Stalin waits then drinks.) Beria, toast our comrade and not on the open fire . . . not yet. Ha.

Beria: Welcome, comrade, to our nightly circus. I mean, circle. Here today gone tomorrow. Drunk or sober, that's life. Nasdrovia!
Kaganovich: I propose a toast to our newest member, comrade Sergeiyevich. We congratulate you on your good work for the party in Georgia.
Stalin: We have a saying in the south, when you ax a tree, the chips will fly.
All: Nasdrovia!
Beria: When Nikta Sergeiyevich sits on your head you know you've been sat on.
Stalin: Was that sits or shits?
Beria: Either way you're fucked! (Laughter.)
Stalin: Give us a toast. Come. Don't be shy. You're among friends, eh, Beria?
Beria: You can depend on us like the weather. (Laughter.)
Sergeiyevich: I don't know what to say.
Stalin: (Angrily.) Then go back to the toilet and think of something. I'll give you a hint, comrade; we're not looking for Lenin's April Theses.
Sergeiyevich: I, ah, have–
Stalin: (Angrily.) Get out! Go! (Suddenly smiling.) Ha, ha. Judging by your face you still had some shit left to be scared out of you.
Beria: Still water runs deep.
Stalin: Sometimes silence is not golden just yellow.
Sergeiyevich: To politicians who are the same everywhere. They promise to build bridges even where there is no water.
All: Nasdrovia!
Stalin: A little leak sinks a great ship.
All: Nasdrovia!
Kaganovich: Petty ills are the fountains of most complaints. Men do not trip on mountains. They stumble on pebbles.
All: Nasdrovia!
Molotov: A toast to the hypocrite. A man who killed his parents then pleaded for mercy saying he was an orphan.
Stalin: That's you, Beria. Nasdrovia!
Beria: To Voyzhid!
Stalin: Yes. To Stalin, serpent of the people.
All: Nasdrovia!

Molotov: (Whispering.) Did he say–
Voroshylov: Don't correct him.
Molotov: Me? Never. I'm not suicidal yet.
Voroshylov: (Standing.) To Stalin, servant of the people!
All: Nasdrovia! (Stalin turns on a record player, dances, and stops.)
Stalin: Age has crept up on me. Sergeiyevich, do that Georgian folk dance. What the hell is it called?
Sergeiyevich: The Gopak.
Stalin: Yes. Let those chubby legs shoot out like a Don Bass peasant. Hey, yah! Spare nothing. Dance!
(All clap and shout as Sergeiyevich dances, squats on his haunches and barely kicks out his heels to everyone's delight; huge applause as he collapses.)
Stalin: No. This is how it goes. (He dances around to applause.) Beria, come. Give us a show. Yes. Good. Da, da! (Beria dances others join in doing solos.)
Sergeiyevich: I must be in the office early. Thank you. Good night every–.
Stalin: Dance, comrade. Dance! This is how we get to know each other, drink breaking bread, and dancing. So, dance. Everyone. Tomorrow you sit. Tonight you dance. Dance, you sons–a–bitches! Dance! Hey–yah! Dance! Tomorrow we may all be dead.
Stalin: Sergeiyevich, try the giblets. They are superb.
Sergeiyevich: Yes. Tasty. Delicious. (Stalin watches then eats.)
Stalin: This is a new bottle of wine, Molotov. Open it. Drink. Is it good?.
Molotov: Exceptional, Boss. (Stalin drinks.)
Stalin: Kaganovich, why do you look away when I look at you?
Kaganovich: I'm looking for giblets.
Stalin: You don't look me in the eye. Is something on your mind you're not telling me? (He nods no.) Good. Drink up. Molotov, how is the herring?
Molotov: Excellent, Voyzhid. Not salty. (Stalin eats.)
Stalin: Voroshylov, try the mushrooms. Good?
Voroshylov: Delicious. (Stalin eats. Beria waves for retainer to bring food.)

Stalin: (Waving for silence; whispering.) Here comes Matryona Petrovna. Quiet. (In the silence she places food before Beria; speaks with thick nasal accent.)

Matryona: Comrade Beria, here is your grass. (Beria eats with his hands.)

Stalin: (Mimicking.) Comrade, Beria. Here is your Grass! Grass! Ha, ha! You eat with your fingers. Are you afraid the utensils are contaminated? But who knows where your fingers have been? You stick them in a lot of pies.

Beria: Fingers cut out the middleman. Indians never use utensils.

Stalin: You're not Indian.

Beria: (Wiggling fingers in the air.) The original chopsticks.

Stalin: You're a leftover from those Asiatic hordes.

Beria: Who's an Asiatic whore?

Stalin: Hordes, Beria. As in barbarics.

Beria: O, the kettle calls the pot black. We're all Chinese. Almond eyes in Slavic clothes. (Pulls out corners of each eye.) Look. (Takes out a pair of chopsticks.)

Stalin: What else is in those pockets, hidden up your sleeves?

Beria: Only my shirt. A toast, comrades, to Voyzhid, a man without prejudice because everyone is suspect. Nasdrovia! (Drinks.)

Stalin: To Beria who always looks twice in the mirror to make sure he's not pulling a fast one on himself. Nasdrovia!

All: Nasdrovia!

Beria: To Kaganovich who counts his money in front of a mirror because he doesn't trust himself. Nasdrovia!

Kaganovich: (Taps glass with spoon.) Gentlemen, gentlemen, what was I going to say? What is the difference? Here is a toast to what I was going to say, and hope I never remember because it was probably a lie anyway.

Stalin: What the hell're you talking about?

Kaganovich: To mamushka, mothers everywhere. Nasdrovia.

Molotov: Mothers are soft, fathers hard.

Kaganovich: My mamushka, my dear old mamushka, Climb up on the stove my son, No longer to rove, my son, Mamushka you've long forgot, but not chicken dumplings in the pot.

All: Climb up on the stove my son. Nasdrovia.
Stalin: (Raising glass.) To Beria's rabbit food. It puts roses on his cheeks and he shits rainbows.
All: Nasdrovia!
Beria: (Rising.) Thank you, beloved comrades. I deserve many toasts, many accolades, but if we toasted all my good work we'd be here–
Stalin: Under five seconds. Get on with it. I'm getting drier by the word. A toast, or is it a secret?
Beria: In other words—(Drunken hooting.)
Stalin: What words? Out with it.
Beria: In other words, my drunken comatose comrades–
Kaganovich: In other words. (Foot stomping by all.)
Beria: Raise your glasses high. Higher!
Stalin: Are we drinking or the ceiling?
Beria: Here's to less sentiment and more victims.
All: Nasdrovia!
Stalin: To Beria who sleeps with one eye open.
Beria: Two. My servant sleeps for me. We shall all sleep soon enough.
Stalin: What's that you say?
Beria: Like you said, Voyzhid. Tomorrow we may all be dead. We're born to die. Not you, of course. You were born for other things.
Stalin: What things, you drunken sot?
Beria: To put iron in Russian backs, to show American cowboy movies, and to get us drunk as skunks.
Stalin: You had a head start before you got here. Beria, you phony Georgian bastard. You were weaned on a bottle of vodka. Wait. Silence. Listen. Do you hear it? (Beat.) That's Beria thinking. Did you know Beria was a caesarean baby? His mother took one look and had a seizure. Ha, ha. (Silence.) That's funny! Right? Ha, ha.
All: Dah. Hilarious. Ha, ha, ha.
Beria: That's pitiful.
Stalin: When the joke is on us it is always bad. Those who laughed had better watch out. I know who is genuine and who is not. You're all fresh faces. When I collaborated with Lenin on "Marxism and the National Question", the old man's notion of a

socialist state, he said, *Koba, you're my wonderful Georgian.* Sure. I could type faster than him. He goes, *Koba, Archimedes said, Give me a fulcrum and I'll move the earth.* (Foot stomping.) We had that in common, a desire to move the earth. When the old man died I found that fulcrum. (Stops short of saying too much.) You parasitical mealy mouths have to get up early to fool me. Don't think I don't know what you're up to. You're making goddamn fortunes. You have cars, dachas. I know how much money is running through your slimy fingers, you Janus–faced scoundrels! Beria, why do you look away?

Beria: I'm searching for Indians. Scalps! Woo! Woo!

Stalin: I'm going to scalp you. (Grabs a knife.)

Beria: (Grabs a knife.) I'm scalping Molotov. (A chase ensues.)

Stalin: (Stops; drops knife; sits.) Beria. You're the devil's disciple. I don't know what Russia would do without you. Probably sleep better at night. Next to you Yezhov is a choirboy. To capitalists: The more they speak of honor and justice the faster we count our spoons. Nasdrovia!

All: Nasdrovia! (Lights out.)

Scene 3

Death of Lenin and Alleluyeva

Place: Bedroom of Stalin's country dacha.

Time: Just returned from an interrupted dinner at Voroshylov's home.

Svetlana: Sometimes I wonder who am I really? Certainly not my father's daughter, biologically, yes, but as I get older I feel I am more like my mother, at least I hope so. Mother was a gentle soul not given to impertinence, I am told, not interested in politics, and somewhat naïve, an innocent in a den of vipers. Over the years, but especially towards the end, father talked incessantly about mother to the point of driving me crazy. Mother was younger than father and devoted to him. In the early days of their marriage mother had been a student at the Moscow Institute. She would travel back and forth from the Kremlin to the institute not in a private car as she might've easily done, but by public conveyance so as not to draw attention to herself. Her fellow students didn't know she was Stalin's wife. In time she began to hear things, as I did, rumors of terrible things father had supposedly done. At first she pretended not to hear them even denied their validity, but the talk persisted and upset mother who had a fine disposition and a sensitive nature. She started asking father if there was any truth in them. He dismissed it as gossip and lies. One night they were having dinner at Voroshilov's house and mother brought up the subject of atrocities. In a rare show of emotion father exploded, pulled her away angrily. At home he became irate, and violent, according to one of the servants.

Stalin: Why suddenly all these questions?

Alliuyeva: (Distraught.) Sudden to you not to me. I have been hearing things.

Stalin: You started at Voroshylov's embarrassing me before guests. I say stop and you're at it again. What things?

Alliuyeva: They say there is famine in the countryside–

Stalin: Nadya–

Alliluyeva: The result of your policies. How can you ignore it?

Stalin: Are you deaf and dumb? You started at Voroshylov's embarrassing me. I asked you to stop then and now, but you don't. You continue to persist.

Svetlana: A student's father was taken away in the middle of the night. She hasn't seen him in months.

Stalin: Police business. I don't know.

Alliluyeva: At school they say you terrorize your colleagues? Is that true?

Stalin: You're there for studies not rumor mongering.

Svetlana: Why don't you answer? They say you poisoned Lenin. (Beat.) They say you had him isolated and denied access to him even to his wife. They say you burned Lenin's intestines to destroy the evidence.

Stalin: (Calmly.) Don't you see what is going on? They are using you to get to me, to destroy me. They will go to extremes to do it. They are afraid to confront me directly and so they plant crazy ideas in your head. This I resent. The hand of Nadya Krupskaya is back of all this traitorous blabbering nonsense, she and those lying subversive Trotskyites. Well, I'll fix them all. She will find herself even more isolated. I've got a woman who will come forward as Lenin's real wife, and that will stop her wagging tongue. In fact she is long overdue for a vacation. Now, what I want from you is the names of those talkative students.

Alliluyeva: I don't know them personally.

Stalin: Yet you trust their word?

Alliluyeva: I'm merely asking if there is validity to what they say.

Stalin: I'm going to send them all packing, the whole institute off to the gulags. You don't understand what it takes to rule. They only talk now, but tomorrow they may act. The trick is to nip them in the bud. Stop. Not another word. The subject is closed. Don't talk. Don't say another word.

Alliluyeva: I received an anonymous letter describing your capacity for vindictive behavior. (To audience.) One day in 1927 Trotsky left the Kremlin to go home. Walking along the street he saw three girls playing. He patted them on the head and walked on. After Trotsky was expelled from Russia, Stalin killed each of those girls.

Stalin: Ha, ha. Trotskyite falderal.

Alliluyeva: Did you poison Lenin? It's written on the Kremlin wall.

Stalin: What else is written?

Alliluyeva: Lenin's death was the start of Stalin's climb to power.

Stalin: Listen. Forget it. Understand? Go to bed.

Alliluyeva: How did Lenin die? Why does it upset you to talk–?

Stalin: Stop! Goddamnit! Go to bed. They're trying to get to me through you. They don't dare say it to my face. You should've said, tell my husband. Say it to his face. They'd sing a different tune then. (Beat.) I went into Lenin's room, he asked for tea, I turned, poured him a glass, and when I turned back he was gone. Just like that. The official medical report said, *Death from cerebral hemorrhage.* What else could we say? The truth would've destroyed the party.

Alliluyeva: What is the truth?

Stalin: Russia needs Russian heroes. Once when the pain was unbearable he begged me for poison.

Alliluyeva: O, God!

Stalin: Not God. Me So–so. He died from something else, something he—never mind. The man was incapacitated, a vegetable. I pushed him along.

Alliluyeva: (Pulling away.) What have I done with my life?

Stalin: You had none before me. I took you from shit and gave you a life in the Kremlin. (Shoves her.) Do you take me for some second rate bureaucrat? Eh? It's no Sunday school picnic leading that pack of wolves.

Alliluyeva: They say you're the devil incarnate.

Stalin: (Moves down C.) Lenin and Trotsky did their share of killing. In 1922 Lenin had a stroke, suffered paralysis in his arm and leg, could no longer take part in the daily administration of the party. That's when the struggle for power within the party surfaced then intensified after his death in 1924. Lines were drawn, groups formed and reformed. It was evident to me that those intellectual blockheads would rather argue than act. Well, I acted. (Drinks; stumbles.) Don't bother going to school anymore. It's already a desert. People will wonder if it ever existed. There is no room in my heart for anything but unquestioned obedience. Nothing comes before my will including you. Those Trotskyites will pay for this. (Kicks chair.) Lenin died because it was his time—Understand?—How and why doesn't matter. Fanya shot Lenin. He shrugged it off like a joke, but he was never the same afterward. Who knows what other devils were at work undetected? It was–Well, Lenin's close associates were Jews. Fanya was a Jewess. Russia needs Russian leaders and Russian idols, not separatist Jews. The Jews killed Lenin. Russia needs its idols untainted and super–human. Russians are hard people. They'd never follow a weak, and tarnished mortal. Wake up, woman. Lenin was mortal, passionate, and that cow of a wife couldn't fill his needs, or bare children. Her thyroid condition rendered her sexless. I heard it from the horse's mouth. Women need affection. Men need release. Lenin had needs. He didn't spend all his time in libraries. I have only two hands, but when it comes to people I don't like I have ways of multiplying them tenfold. Nadya, Lenin's hag, came to visit him on his deathbed. (Drunken mimicry.) *Good eve–ning, comb–raid.* I go, what the hell's good about it? Where do you think you're going *to shee my hus–band.* Sorry, bug eyes, no visitors. What is that you say? Doctor's orders. No visitors. *My visiting rights*—Get the fuck out of here! You have no rights. *You're treading on thin ice, comb—raid. Move away.* (Mimes blocking her.) *I'm his wife!* Ha. Ha!! In bed you were this close. (Puts up three fingers, points to middle one.) That's Inessa in the middle. *O, you vulgar man. How dare you? I didn't join the Party yesterday.* You're a relic good only for dick–tation. *You nasty, filthy, rude—O, when Ilych hears of this you'll be sorry.* The man can't see, can't talk, or lift a finger. Get the hell out of here, you pop eyed cow! (Segue to.)

Cameo

(Lurking in the shadows; mumbling as she reenacts shooting Lenin.)

Fanya: Listen to the silence. What? Shh. Listen. The silence. O, quit the crap. We've been silent too long. Here's your silence. (Brandishing gun.) The only silence people understand. Where's the winery? Smolney, Savnarkin? Silence! When Lenin turns the corner. We get what we deserve. Listen, the gun, the bullets. Listen to them. They're focused and ready. I am. I'm trying. To focus. You keep talking. The bullets are ready. Quiet. Hear that? The clink of deutchamarks. What? The bullets are dipped and loaded. You're dipped and loaded. Yes. Full of poison, too. The silence has a pulse. Shh. That's him. No. God, I feel a chill up my spine. That's all very well, but your goddamn silence doesn't put bread on the table. Bread? Yes. Bread. You can't eat silence and glory. The only food I need is truth. Truth is sustenance. Death is starvation, yes, and too good for that bastard. When Lenin turns the corner of Smolny Institute—There he is with a comrade. Definitely that's him. Yes. Go. Now. Do it. Die. Crumble and die. Mark it August 1918. All that ran through my head. (Walking.) Steady now. Steady. Easy. A little closer. Just a few steps. Now! *Heir Lenin! What? This!* Boom! Boom! He fell. I ran. I should put another bullet in his head. But no need. Go. Get out of here. If the bullets don't kill him the poison will. *Long Lives the Revolution! Traitor to the cause!* As I ran I thought no more peccadilloes for that double–dealing bastard! Later, the news reported he was shot but alive. What? Alive? O, God! No. Can't be. But it was true. How, why, who knows? I just sunk down and cried.

Lenin: When Civil War ended in 1921 I implemented our New Economic Policy (NEP), or collective farming. The farmers and peasants rebelled and refused to work land that they could not hand down to their children. I realized that they were not ready to grasp basic socialism, and so I reinstated private ownership of the land by the peasants, but kept big industry under state control. In 1922 I had the first of several fatal strokes culminating in a fatal "cerebral hemorrhage" in 1924.

Fanya: (Shouting.) Lies! Lies! Dora Fanya, radical revolutionary, call me Fanny. Let's cut to the quick, comrades. I shot you in the shoulder and neck August 1918.

Lenin: I took it as a joke and laughed it off.

Fanya: The joke was on the people. One bullet was removed, the other left in because it was in a (Mockingly.) *sensitive area too deep to risk extracting*. They should've let me operate and I'd gladly say, the operation was a success, but the patient died. The whole business was strange. Bullets laced with poison and neither one killed him. Go figure that? Why?

Voices: He was built like a bull. Exercised a lot. Could do a hundred pushups.

Fanya: Lenin knows. Speak up, com–rade. Debunk the big cover–up. Cat got your tongue? Stalin knows. That lunatic knows about things before they happen. *Whom the Gods would destroy they first make mad.*

Scene 4

Place: Lenin's bedroom, Kremlin.

Time: Same as scene 1.

Lenin: (Becoming delirious.) I itch all over. Oo, scratching makes it worse. The sheets are like led. I can't stand the pain. Kill me. You are the one to do it. The others are sentimental. (Stalin nearby fixing tea.) Afterward, burn me. No one will be wiser. Strange. This awful trick, this devilish quirk of nature. It gives and takes. My life has been a race against time. Get me a gun, Koba, a bullet to end it. Inessa? Where is my blue notebook? The devil you say, Sasha! Ha! Queen takes knight. *Kindly oblige us with your absence.* I must tell the Congress.

Stalin: They've adjourned.

Lenin: (Slurring words.) I want to a–address them, tell them to be gentle with each other, appreciate what we have achieved. O, these goddamn sheets, and the itching. I can't hold a pencil to write. What good is a man who can't hold a pencil and write? A man who can't write is dangerous. Sasha, set up the board. Is it true father will never come home again? I'll help with the samovar.

Stalin: We all die sooner or later. For some sooner is better.

Lenin: (Twisting about.) O, these sheets are scorching. I need a cool spot. Do what you must do as one comrade to another. Understand me, what I am saying? We're just in the vestibule. Do you understand? One or two steps more and—Goddamnit! (Twisting.) Impossible to get comfortable. What is most painful is the race between life and death, to be unable to finish, to be incapacitated at the doorstep by an invisible devil of blind fate. Smaller than a mote yet mightier than the sword, *Abandon all hope yee who enter here.* Fulcrum.

Stalin: What?

Lenin: I had leverage, Inessa. About to *move the earth!*

Stalin: I am your fulcrum. Your tea, Voyzhid.

Lenin: Leave nothing to venerate. Do not raise my picture. Raise high the workers peek cap. Aye! If I could I would go through these walls and destroy every last wrong, every—don't let what we've done fall to nothing. Koba, all work and no play makes for a dull . . . (Lapsing into delirium Inessa appears.) You come bringing lilacs. I drink you in like spring sunshine.

Inessa: When you have all the symptoms the disease doesn't matter.

Lenin: The symptoms.
Inessa: Ilych, truth and death are twins. In between flows a river and the naked lady of the lilacs stoops to glimpse herself, something fantastic shimmering in the river, a vision of self in the river, naked–
Lenin: Innocence passing on. (Gorky fades in and out.)
Gorky: In your mouth words were like the cold glint of steel shavings. Your sentences thrown out like blocks of hewn granite. (Fades away.)
Lenin: What does it all mean? A second ago yesterday was vital. Fifty years gone in the twinkle of an eye. What does it all mean?
Inessa: What we had is what it means.
Lenin: What happened to the music?
Inessa: Get the nets and let's hunt butterflies. There is no rancor in heaven.
(Dissolve to red burning fire and rolling snare drums.)
Nadya: Lenin's contribution to Soviet Russia is the deconstruction of an outmoded imperialism, a bourgeois government, and the introduction of the first stages of a socialist–communist state. My husband put his own life second to that end. In our farewell to a great comrade I ask on his behalf to keep your grief minimal, not to envy or copy him, but to seek your own way in fulfilling what he started. He would not want you to raise his picture or worship him as a spiritual leader, but to devote yourselves to perfecting and building on what has been achieved. In the new Russia there is no room for idolatry, and veneration, or personality cults. There is only room for sharing in common the fruits of our labor. *Do not let your grief be expressed in outward honors for Lenin by designing icons, monuments, and mausoleums to him, or conducting grand pageantry to celebrate him. Such things meant little to him and he found such behavior bourgeois, irksome, and a total waste of precious time and energy. But rather lead your lives stoically as he led his by considering what still must be done, correcting the poverty and disorder that continues in Russia. That is where he would want you to devote your lives. He would say do not raise my picture. Honor me and yourselves by building schools, hospitals, crèches, and homes for children, libraries, sanatoriums for the infirm, and science laboratories dedicated to abolishing illness, and making life's*

struggle easier. Above all Lenin would want you to live life in a way that through you his will is done. Ilych died too soon to witness the success of the new social order in the USSR—if one can call it that. It was well underway until one man changed everything we stood for and had achieved. This is Lenin's last testament to the politburo composed of his inner circle. (Cross fade to Lenin.)

Lenin: Stalin is disrespectful to his colleagues, and should not hold a position of authority within the Party. He should be immediately ostracized. I consider that which is said to my wife, or done to my colleagues, as something also said and done against me. Therefore, Stalin owes me, and my wife an apology . . . In spite of Stalin no power on earth can deprive us of what we have gained through the Russian Revolution. States have organized for hundreds of years in the bourgeois style. For the first time in history a non–bourgeois state has been constructed. Maybe it's not perfect, neither was the first steam engine. Possibly it didn't work even blew up. The point is . . . now we have steam engines. However bad our state apparatus is an important historical invention has been made; a proletarian kind of state has been created. Let all the bourgeois newspapers world–over carry the news about our poverty and sufferings–still the world is drawn to the soviet state because it is the first time in history that the people have triumphed over government and the privileged class. In Russia the land is yours, freedom, and justice is yours. One step forward two steps back but in the end we shall conquer the hearts of all human beings. We shall take back what we have given and reinvest the rights of kings in ourselves. (Cross fade to:)

Svetlana: According to the official statement mother committed suicide. They said it was *an act out of recurring despair. Was it accidental?* Father knows. Did he lose his temper, had he become so enraged that he'd do such a thing to his wife, to my mother? I've since come to be believe what others have known for a long time that father was capable of anything. I know mother was worn out by fits of melancholy, but suicide didn't seem possible. After her death father banned all talk about mother. He cleared the house of all memory of her and it was as though she never existed. He would lapse into melancholy, became sullen and short tempered. No one dared mention mother again in his presence. Then, toward the end, father started talking about mother, desperately seeking the reason for her death. It is possible that his defense was a sublimation of the truth, of the guilt he felt about what really happened. He never revealed himself to anyone, or ever showed signs of remorse about anyone or anything he had done in his life, except about mother. Her death bothered him more than he realized. He cut off relations with anyone who'd seen her that day, that week. I don't think it was sublimation, but rather his way of dealing with life. Father initiated lots of terrible things none of them traceable to him. Afterward, he would sit back, relax and indulge himself in what he called the sweet act of revenge. There is little doubt that he initiated the death of Kirov who was sent to Petersburg to ease the restive mood in 1934. Kirov was well known and liked by everyone, which is why my father sent him away from Moscow and the politburo. He saw Kirov as a rival in the party. Kirov's death was necessary to set the groundwork for the "purge trials" of 1936–1938 ostensibly to rid the party of subversives, but in truth father had wanted to eliminate Lenin's old guard, the intelligent ones who remembered his role in the early days of the revolution. Maybe mother's death and that of Kirov's were catalysts to justify purging "undesireables." He was a consummate innocent and people bought it. I did, but then I was a child.

Stalin: Why did she turn against me? Somebody was feeding her lies. It was Molotov's pea brain Polina who gave her the gun. Why? They caused her to fear for her life, put a grain of doubt in her head, and that was all she needed to see trouble lurking around every corner, assassins hiding in shadows.

Svetlana: Later, I put it all together.

Stalin: That vile book your mother was reading before she died, The Green Hat, affected her. Polina Molotov, Aunt Anna and Pavel—Pavlushka brought the pistol to her. That miserable little pistol. (Forms pistol hand.) Such a miserable little thing, a toy gun, yes, something a child would use playing cops and robbers. Polina I'll fix her. They'll get what's coming to them.

Svetlana: The louder father's protestations the more was his sense of guilt. At first I couldn't believe it, but it was true to

father's character to initiate horrors then play innocent. Father was a great actor.
(Stalin and daughter talk back forth while she addresses the audience.)
Stalin: I gave your mother more than she ever dreamed of possessing. How could she do this to me?
Svetlana: To you? What about Mother?
Stalin: It's a black mark on my reputation. If I can't control my wife how can I control a country? Trust someone see where it gets you? She dishonored me.
Svetlana: I was in the room when father was dying, strictly in the background, never approaching his bed. What could I say to this man, my father, who had ruined so many lives? I was there because it was the Christian thing to do. At his side were the members of his inner circle, the fawners and sycophants. Before the end father's eyes had been closed for a time. Beria leaned in thinking father had expired, saying, *he is not breathing. He's dead. At last the tyrant is dead.* He cackled and started to give orders. Suddenly father opened his eyes and a shocked Beria reversed himself with platitudes of joy and praises of thanks. Father looked at Beria with enmity and contempt. He looked at everyone with what seemed to me accusatory and suspicious eyes that said, I know you poisoned me; you're not fooling me. His eyes turned yellow the color of a snake with hues of brown and seemed to express venom and regret that he no longer had the power to control, or to kill them. (Lights down and up on:)
Stalin: It was nothing but a toy. Pavlushka gave it to her. A fine thing to give anybody. Who was guilty? Who put her up to it? Those sniveling Trotskyites.
Svetlana: Father looked everywhere for culprits but at himself to shift the blame to some outside enemy: the Bund, the sniveling Mensheviks.
Stalin: People in the commissariat, the chauffeur, the cooks. Polina, Molotov's wife, was a bad influence on your mother.
Svetlana: Some time later Polina was sent to Siberia, and Molotov was never again invited into the inner circle. Father refused to consider more valid reasons, things that made their life together so hard. He looked for simple direct causes, as though that was

all there was to it. Mother had been a party group organizer at the Industrial Academy; studied chemistry in the textile factory, specializing in artificial fibers. Father chastised mother for swallowing gossip. In time she believed the ghastly rumors of deaths and disappearances and it affected her.
Stalin: Then there was that goddamn book The Green Hat!
Svetlana: I saw by his behavior he had long ago lost the memory of what my mother was really like. Pushkin wrote *you don't hitch a horse and a quivering doe to the same cart.* If mother's life was like mine no wonder she gave up. Whenever I travel and the train pulls into a station I go for a stroll along the platform, walk as far as the engine, greet the workmen, but never see a single passenger.
Stalin: It was my private train for your safety. No one was allowed near it.
Svetlana: The platform deserted and sinister, sad, and depressing, and I suffered as a prisoner of your system. I was stifling from loneliness, emptiness, and lack of human companionship.
Stalin: Try to understand, Svetka. My enemies could get to me through you.
Svetlana: It's interesting that father and Beria should have a sense of humor. There is nothing funny about how they did business yet there are moments of humor. General Vlasik and a colonel were head of father's bodyguard. They were both fat from cognac and self–importance at state expense. Father would grind his teeth and insult them with crude words. He never talked that way to his household servants. At 72 father walked along with a brisk stride with that fat general and the bodyguard panting behind him to keep up. Suddenly, he would change course, run into them, explode with anger, and scold the one nearest him on any trivial pretext. Father indulged his feelings privately, but outwardly he'd say *that's for women.* He hated applause and crowds, had forgotten that feelings could be sincere. The real Stalin became all too obvious even to himself and this was not pleasant.
Stalin: "Cosmopolitan"? (Signaling someone off.) Arrest all "cosmos."
Svetlana: Such bitterness against the whole world. The years solidified into an unavoidable truth: the old must give way to the new. Youth with its resilience and dynamism, self–absorbed and

egocentric, was no longer his providence. It belonged to a new generation with its own agenda. He found no comfort in leaning back because there was nothing there he could rely on. He'd killed it all in the fight for power. I never heard father utter one regret, show one sign of remorse about anything. When it came to emotions he had bolted himself behind an impenetrable steel door. He'd done unspeakable things, beat all the odds against a semi–educated man rising to lead the greatest land empire on earth. He learned from Lenin that sympathy and compassion belong to children like the fairy tales in the bible. What he took from the bible and seminary school was simple: vanquish your enemy by any means. As Marc Antony said, *the good is oft buried with the dead, but the evil lives on.* Early on father developed a dislike for emotional displays, for things that might make him feel lowly, and so he beat back everything that came in his path, destroyed anyone showing the slightest gift, a modicum of superiority. He once said, we all get what we deserve. Under my father that meant what he decided we deserved. Yagoda, Yezhov, Beria were all extensions of father, especially Beria who fed father's paranoia, and was the guiltier one in many crimes. His hand was back of all the murders of innocent comrades. Towards the end even father began to fear Beria might try to kill him. So father drank to drown out the ghosts of what he'd done. Old age angered father because he couldn't stop it with a wave of the hand. In father's final hours I felt he was defiant, grappling with death in a losing battle, which he refused to give up. I have no doubt that his soul is still battling death with that same misanthropic disposition he held in life.

Stalin: Even you make anti soviet statements. How does that make me look?

Svetlana: Curiosity is not necessarily subversive, father. At least that is how I tried to answer him. Father showed little weakness or remorse, but inside he felt what he'd done, and rationalized what happened. The real Stalin became all too obvious even to himself and this was not pleasant.

Stalin: They open their mouths and yell like fools.

Svetlana: Powerful as he was he was impotent in the face of the frightful system that had grown up around him and he was helpless to either destroy it or bring it under control. It is staggering to think what he had done. My father was guilty of monstrous crimes with accomplices. He victimized millions of Soviet citizens and hundreds of thousands more in neighboring countries who feared invasion or sudden abduction at night without warning.

Stalin: I love in order to hate more cunningly, to undo, to kill you, your innocence, in little matters day–to–day under the guise of love and ill temper. I take your goodness, your blood and destroy your initiative. It suits me, feeds my empty soul. So it's more than a question of self–aggrandizement? Let's say—it's not that every Jew has his Jew or that rivalry between family members is based on jealousy and envy. No. It's deeper than egotism. It's hatefulness. People hate each other. Given the chance to act with impunity they'll destroy each other. Long ago I decided to act first. Kill or be killed. Pure and simple. I trusted no one. The very idea of trust is suicidal. It amounts to stepping into a bed of snakes thinking you won't get bitten. So I concluded when there's doubt, where there is intelligence namely competitive spirit, snuff it out before it gets you. Kill the man you kill the problem . . . When I woke up late the next day I could not find my wife. I wanted to talk, have a little something to eat and talk. In life so many things come and go. One is pulled in so many directions, that little things get lost and later become big things. I wanted to clear the air, touch her, and do something I rarely ever do, apologize for my behavior. A man in my position can't go around apologizing. It's a sign of weakness. But for her, I make an exception. God! If only I knew what drives me so mad. Why do I take offense at the drop of a hat? I thought, well, patience. She's gone for a walk. Then, something told me, no, something drew me to her private room in another part of the dacha. And that's where I found her. (Pauses; almost emotional.) I couldn't believe what I saw. I stood looking at her and couldn't believe it. In bed, head on the pillow, blood everywhere, my wife's blood. I looked around for a villain, some treachery. The gun was by the bed near her hand. Suicide? No. Not my wife. Do that? How could she? Where did she get the guts to do that to me, Stalin? Stalin! Nobody does that to me. I say who lives and dies. (Turns up L, sits; follow spot on Svetlana stage R.)

Svetlana: My father felt mother's "suicide" posed more of an embarrassment to him than loss of a wife. He locked himself in his study and did not come out for a long time. I don't think he ever cried over my mother. Like so many things in his life, he kept it locked inside of him. (Calling out.) Father? Are you in there? Are you awake, father? (Silence.) If he grieved he never shared it with me, or my brother, or anyone, never spoke of it once, in private or public. Mother had betrayed him pure and simple and he tore her from his life like a page from a book and lived as though mother never existed. From that time on he became morose and inner–directed. No one could get near him. He left a lot of things to Lavrenti Beria who, in defense of father, was often the bigger culprit.

Mamushka: (Gavels.) I think it is safe to conclude your father was a suspicious man. Then how did Beria win your father's confidence?

Svetlana: Father was going on a trip south. Before departing Beria went ahead in secret and sawed the pilings of a bridge along the travel route. Later, when Stalin's caravan approached that bridge, Beria said, stop. Let's be sure the bridge is safe. Father sent one of the cars up ahead to check it out, and the bridge collapsed.

Mamushka: Naturally, Beria won Stalin's respect. Go on.

(Light on Stalin seated in rocking chair smoking a pipe.)

Svetlana: Father was a cynical realist. He had a sober, practical low view of life He developed in seminary school a non–spiritual outlook stemming from the hypocracy and two–facedness–.

Mamushka: Typical of the clergy. Well, some of them.

Svetlana: The lack of compromise, inflexibility, inability to agree with opposing opinion, I attribute to his experience at the seminary.

Stalin: I never speak of my father. He is an embarrassment. His treatment of my mother—well, if it were today I would nail his drunken shoemaker ass to a last. This arm is shorter than the other. A result of my father's brawling drunkenness, slapping, kicking my mother in the belly while I was yet unborn. Distrust, indifference to people came naturally to me the way it does to snakes and cats. I strike without remorse, or the need to gloat publicly. In private I do get a rush of personal satisfaction and that suffices. After a kill animals do not throw a party and toast the deceased. I do party only no one knows it but me. Some people are born with native talents: Trotsky was a writer by instinct turned politician–warrior, but in a clinch he lacked the skill of close quarter in-fighting, and clung to the illusion of allegiances. He never understood that he was obnoxious, and condescending, and that people do not forgive offense to their pride. Tell them the truth and they will despise you. His haughtiness made enemies. I capitalized on it. While he kept people at a distance, I drew them near. While he corrected them, I encouraged them. He gave them his tongue. I gave them my ear. He fathered them while I mothered them. Ultimately a mother's influence always wins out because fathers are hard and mothers are soft. I kept them close to the tit, dependant, beholding. I created a party within a party, my own private cadre of children tied to my apron strings. At the slightest sign of independence or individuality, I cut them loose, setting one against the other. Oh, but it was fun to watch. To strike fear in a comrade, that his job, his family and all his dreams might end in a flash—that could create the most incredible waffling of position. Torture was the main weapon. It could change a man's mind many times over. Crumble to nothing his sense of himself, his ideals, his opinions. Fear is a wonderful motivator. I've often wondered how a cat feels after playing with a mouse. Is there a sense of accomplishment, or all in a day's work? A rabbit sees a snake stuck in a hole. The snake says, "Help me out and I promise not to bight you." The rabbit says, "Okay," helps the snake out and snake bights him. "But you promised," says the rabbit. "Yes," says the snake. "But I can't help myself. It's my nature." Me? It all crystallized in my mother's womb. I was born to cut through the façade of social amenities, to find out what really propelled individuals, and events. The secret was act, don't reflect. Hesitate and you're dead. What I am was bred in the womb. It's a gift like playing piano. I practice assiduously the way a pianist exercises on the keys, playing people one against the other. Watching them crumble gives me satisfaction. Books don't interest me. I leaf through people, create events, situations, set the animals in motion, and know the outcome before it happens.

Coachie: I have in my troika your Handbook of Philosophy written by Rosenthal and Yudin. The book credits you with writing a series of articles in 1905 "Armed Insurrection and Our Tactics", "Reaction Is Growing", and "Notes of A Delegate", supposedly written on your return from the Fifth Congress in London. I quote, " . . . a masterly defense of the tactical position of Bolshevism." But you were not in the Party at that time. The book would have us believe you were a Bolshevik before the word was coined. In truth you were in the Caucasus involved in criminal acts and banditry. Here, wonder of wonders, the writers say you "developed further" Lenin's theory of the possibility of Socialism in the Soviet Union. You, a non–writer, amplified Lenin's work? Incredible! You did what his peers couldn't, or didn't dare to do. I speak of your intellectual superiors Zinoviev, Kamenev, and Bukharin. By the way what happened to them? (Pause.) In 1936, we are told, you authored "The Constitution of the USSR", and an essay "Dialectical–Historical Materialism" as part of your history of the Communists of the Soviet Union. Marvelous! Of course Maxim Gorky had nothing to do with the Constitution, or the group commissioned to write it in 1933. Let's get down to fundamentals. You inherited certain native skills from the Caucasus mountain peasants schooled in the art of survival. Some who knew you back then said you were a police informer. A document surfaced that incriminates you, but it well may be a forgery. Usually, where there is smoke there is fire.

Stalin: (*Goodby speech.*) I killed to get God's attention. Many times, I thought, look, God, at what I'm doing. See all the dead piled up—women and children and still you do not show yourself? You listening to me? Show yourself. I'm waiting. Nothing. Like always. Here I insult you and you do nothing. What the hell kind of God are you? A nothing God, that's what. To hell with you! Even torture fails to get your attention. You're dead. Reason is dead and history is forever pissing against the waves.

EPILOGUE

Old Guard Talk and A Galician Fiasco

Scene 1

Time–Place: Limbo. Coachie in a blue or red suit with yellow shoes. (Note: Bracketed words delivered by all a performance choice. Stalin visible back of a scrim in a rocker as in a court dock, listening, smoking a pipe.)

Bukharin: An early testament of Lenin's was cautionary advice to the Party: *do not repeat the mistake of the Jacobins.*
Mamushka: Meaning what?
Kerensky: Mutual extermination.
Bukharin: Correct. No death penalty imposed on Party members who express opposing positions. There were isolated exceptions between 1924 and 1930.
Kerensky: Escalating in the 1930's to become the rule not the exception.
Bukharin: In 1932 half of Russia suffered from famine. The dominant opinion blamed Stalin for arousing the peasants against the Party. (Hooting.) A majority in the Central Committee thought that only his removal could save us. Feeling differed in the Politburo. (Boo! Idiots!) The argument was what program would replace Stalin's party line? Among the proposals and declarations circulating, Riutin's programme some two hundred pages was unique for its severe criticism of Stalin—far from flattering—describing him as the "evil genius" of the Russian revolution whose vindictiveness and hunger for power brought the revolution to the edge of the abyss. (Foot stomping.) *Stalin had to be removed* or *there'd be no recovery in the party or the country*—yet no definitive action was taken. Riutin paid dearly for this later on. Stalin got hold of a

copy. This led to arrests and house searches. Anyone connected to Riutin was arrested. At the time Riutin was in an "isolator".

Mamushka: What is an *iso later*?

Rabble Voices: A place of harsh environment. Life with your mother–in–law! (Laughing; foot stomping.)

Mamushaka: (Gaveling.) Order! Another outburst you'll be removed from the bistro. Go on with your story.

Bukharin: As an old Bolshevik who had rendered eminent service to the Party, Riutin came within the sphere of those against whom, in accordance with Lenin's commandment, there could be no question of the death penalty. Stalin's argument in the Politburo was for the OGPU's—(The KGB. Political police. Boo!) Stalin was for their decision to execute Riutin based on increased terrorist sentiment among young people in the Komsomol or Young Communist League. There had been terrorist attacks against party leaders or minor officials. Stalin instigated the rumors and alleged subversive activities pitting people against each other to justify his failure and the famine. (Boo!) His talent was putting people in opposition to one another who then became his victims. It was his way to secure his position. The sort of thing he delighted in that suited his twisted personality. (Foot stomping.)

Kirov: (Rising.) I am Sergei M. Kirov, member of the Politburo, First Secretary of the Communist Party for the Leningrad Province, formerly Petersburg.

Kerensky: Stalin's second–in–command. His chief rival for power.

Kirov: I supported Lenin's edict, *no death penalty* especially to old timers.

Stalin: I valued Kirov. He towed the party line with great energy and loyalty, but . . . there was an annoying independence in his attitude.

Bukharin: Stalin feared Kirov's popularity. He was smart enough not to push matters between them to an open conflict where he'd be on shaky ground, and decided to rely on other means to get his way.

Kerensky: Like what? Be specific.

Bukharin: Deception, murder. (Foot stomping.)

Kirov: I had been re–elected to the Politburo and chosen as secretary of the Central Committee requiring my presence in Moscow.
Stalin: You are needed in Leningrad. You can come back when I find a replacement. (Boo!)
Buckharin: Which never happened. It would've been folly for Stalin to add Kirov to the already large number of the *dissatisfied* and important party leaders. So Stalin waited and plotted his strategy. Kirov was loved, had surrounded himself with devoted and reliable aids. He had enough power to follow his own line.
Kirov: Russia's position in the world necessitated a more open foreign policy in order to keep up with changing times.
Stalin: Internal dissenters besieged The Fatherland. Trotskyites!
Bukharin: Stalin trumped up bogeymen like *la patria in danger,* instilling fear and creating ghosts to divert attention from his failures.
Kirov: I aimed at a Western foreign policy. I was set to create a mighty Russian army to defend against the war with Germany. The writing was on the wall. Germany was building up its military. As to immediate questions of internal politics, I was for abolishing terror, and establishing a proper psychological frame of mind at home. There were two alternatives: Crush dissenters, tighten the pressure ruthlessly thereby antagonizing terror; or take the path of "reconciliation with the people" to gain their voluntary cooperation in preparation for the coming war.
Bukharin: Maxim Gorki was for reconciliation, too, but he was not a member of the Politburo and decision–making. So Kirov's role was critical.
Mamushka: (Gaveling with spoon.) What does the record say?
Kerensky: He was one of the party heads of Stalin's Five–Year Plan, played a big part in the horrors of the Second Five–Year Plan, inspired and implemented notoriously ruthless measures against the peasants and the killing of kulaks. He is not without guilt in the gulag camps, the Kem, and Murmansk wastes.
Kirov: The period of destruction was necessary to extirpate–
Mamushka: Exter–what?

Kirov: Exterminate the small proprietor elements in villages in order to consolidate the economic position of the collectives to secure the future.
Mamushka: While you secured the future for *collectives* Stalin secured the future himself. *Hateful to Mamushka is a man who hides one thing in his heart and speaks another.*
Bukharin: The irony is that people intuitively know the truth yet buy the fairytale. Kirov's assassination–
Mamushka: Extirpation.
Bukharin: In 1934 ended my chance for liberation within the party. The trend was toward intensification of terror inside the party to the point of physical extermination of all those whose party past might make them opponents of Stalin or aspirants to his power. Stalin always protected himself first and foremost by creation of devils, terror, the West, etc. Soon after Kirov died a rumor surfaced that painted him as a Casanova who was shot by a jealous husband. It was in keeping with Stalin's style. Between the murder of Kirov in 1934 and the second Kamenev trial around 1937, Stalin mapped out his future plans: the trial of the "sixteen" and the purges to come, including decimation of our top military leaders, which then left us wide opened for German attack. In fact Hitler admired Stalin's boldness and wished he could do it himself. If a coup is going to come it will be from the military. But for the moment, Stalin understood that the mood of the majority of party workers was bitterness and hostility toward him. The purge trials demonstrated that the party was anti–Stalin. Had Lenin lived Stalin would not have gotten away with it.
Lenin: (Rising.) Absolutely not!
Gallery Voices: He was your expropriator! Your messenger boy! You let him in!
Lenin: I rue that day, comrades. But your memory is short. My last testament cautioned: *Stalin is unsuited to be part of us. He is disrespectful, has the manners of a brute, will only bring us trouble and disgrace. He cannot be relied on to do the right thing.* (Sits arms folded.)
Bukharin: Stalin knew that the old guard rejected him in their hearts. The hostility toward him lay in the basic psychology of the old Bolsheviks. We'd grown up under the conditions of

revolutionary struggle against the old regime and had been trained in the psychology of oppositionists, of irreconcilable non–conformists. Involuntarily our minds work in a direction *critical* of the existing order; we seek everywhere its weakness. We are all critics, destructionists—not builders. As outsiders it was ok, but as insiders we had to occupy ourselves with constructive building, and it was bad.

Lenin: It's impossible to build anything enduring with skeptics and critics.

Bukharin: Stalin built a case for his actions based on self–preservation first–not as he claimed to protect the party and Russia from terrorists or war on the horizon. In an odd way there was logic to his paranoia. If the "old guard" (Lenin's original cadre), the group constituting the new ruling caste in the country, is unfit to perform it's function of war, and building solidarity among the people then it is necessary to remove them and create a new ruling caste. Obviously in an "if" scenario A leads to B and your thinking is correct, but his premise was self–serving. He trumped up devils then played hero by knocking them down, but those devils were in his mind. He bullied those around him to do his bidding out of fear of losing their own situation.

Kirov: My plan presupposed reconciliation with non–party intellectuals. It enlisted non–party workers and peasants in the tasks of socio–political life, as a means of widening the social basis of the Soviet regime and promoting its cooperation with the democratic elements of the population.

Bukharin: Under Stalin's plan these same proposals took a different meaning. They were to facilitate a complete revision of the ruling caste by expelling those infected with the spirit of criticism; then substituting a new personnel governed by a new psychology aimed at positive construction. The old Bolsheviks with a noted revolutionary past ended up hiding in their lairs, trembling. Ironically, we became the enemy. Anyone who crossed the path of a person under investigation–his fate was sealed. No one dared talk to, be seen nears us, or dared to defend us. Simultaneously, Stalin gave the general public all sorts of benefits loosening restrictions. The purpose of it was deliberate: let the memory of our crucifixion be inextricably bound in the minds of the people with the improvements they have received from Stalin. Very sly, and clever. Absolutely masterful. Stalin had us all beat hands down when it came to recrimination. We existed based on his whims. If he could've killed everybody and survived he would've done it. History, I fear, repeats itself. Inequality serves a necessary function in all societies. War is a prime example of inequality. The drones, the poor and uneducated serve as canon fodder, while the rich and educated remain in relative safety back home. Stalin emphasized what Lenin merely suggested. Stalin maneuvered those who held to the old official policy into a position where they appeared to be deviators in violation of Articles 8, or 11: carrying charges like member in a terrorist group, and Non–denunciation, not reporting negative remarks about Stalin and the Party. Even silence was subversive. The difference between Stalinism and a traditional socialist outlook lay in their respective attitudes towards the role of force in the transformation of society. *A Stalin* was a *necessary consequence* of the effort of a minority to keep power and carry out a vast social–economic revolution in a short time. Marxism alluded to force as necessary in changing the old order to the new as in the French revolutions, the American Revolution and Civil War. Force renders the desire, the cry for change from theory and cheap talk to the reality of a visceral experience, which no amount of talk can satisfy. Economics and social processes primarily condition the basic fortunes of people. Force in this regard is limited. Lenin and Marx were optimistic about the future but in minor degrees. Force, and I paraphrase Marx, is the midwife of every old society pregnant with a new one. The mid–wife facilitates birth, gets baby to exit the womb. After that the midwife is not needed. Force according to Stalin as seen in his deeds springs from totalitarians. Stalin represents the old Marx aphorism: Force is no longer the midwife. Force is the mother of the new society.

Kerensky: When Kirov was murdered you must've suspected Stalin.

Bukharin: The Left and Right while disagreeing on economic policy understood that violence was no answer and that in the end compromise is the answer. It was unthinkable that a colleague could be so rancorous, petty, and a total misanthrope.

I said privately to Kemenev, our differences are nothing compared to Stalin. He's an unprincipled intriguer, subordinates everything to his appetite for power, will flip–flop on his position at the drop of a pin in order to destroy a colleague. His political line is bringing us to the great abyss. He's ambitious and hungry for power. Anyone who gets in his way he will eliminate. As for you and me, given the chance he will strangle both of us. Following the assassination of Kirov by Nikolayev, a Stalin henchman, the insidious "Purge Trials" began. In the end Yegoda and Yezhov, chiefs of the murderous secret police, got what they dished out, a bullet in the head. Having done their master's bidding they could bare witness against him. Stalin never liked *loose ends*. Many comrades with superior intellects to Stalin, commonly referred to as Lenin's *old guard*, also had to go: Zinoviev, Kamenev, Rydek, Rykov, Trotsky, all falsely accused by Vyshinsky, Stalin's puppet prosecutor, of attempting to restore capitalism, assassination of Politburo members, wrecking the military and economic power of the country, and trying to poison Stalin.
Kerensky: We know Lenin's legacy is Stalin, the Tasmanian devil. Death and destruction of the human spirit, unwarranted incarcerations of innocent people, and senseless murder. When the fear and paranoia subside, time will distance historians. The archives will open up. Truth will have its day. (Whirling.) Roll over you dead dogs. Debate your way out of hell, if you can.

Scene 2

(Trotsky with notebook in search of truth, besieged by haunts emerging from the shadows. Music: Emperor's Waltz danced with a mix of grace and sudden aggressive, or explosive martial arts moves.)
Trotsky: What a handy tool is the pencil, graphite with an eraser. (Dances.) A weapon ready to commit and erase.
Stalin: (Enter dancing.) You commit, I erase.
Lenin: (Dancing in.) Not having a good day, Leon? Look at me! Light as a bird.
(Enter dancing; singing.)

Bogdanov and Lunacharsky: Incidentally. Not only that.
Trotsky: So many thoughts dancing in my head, variations on themes, intimations of disconnected experiences, emotions riding subtle breezes.
Mamushka: What the hell is he talking about?
Trotsky: Finding the right word is like pulling teeth.
Stalin: Give me a toothpick and a steamroller. (Sits behind scrim smoking.)
Trotsky: One day we'll go madly in an apocalyptic fiery nightmare of gargoyles, griffins, reptiles, and molten lava. (Crumples paper.)
Mamushka: (Waving spoon.) Talk plain, or you'll sit by the door—all of you.
Lenin: Words are coquettes hard to nail down.
Nadya–Inessa: Long in the tooth. Even when you don't know what you're talking about. Still one tries. Nonetheless. To express oneself with a certain etcetera, etcetera. He does have a certain élan about him.)
(Tsar–Tsarina waltz in followed by Felix holding a gun, and then Rasputin.)
Mamushka–Coachie: (Waltzing in.) However. In addition to that.
Lunacharsky–Bogdanov: In other words. I know that.
Trotsky: Enough! You're crowding my head. (Silence.) The Politburo offered me the Chairmanship of the Party. I turned it down. I didn't want people to think the coup was a Jewish conspiracy.
Tsar: Dead leaves under the bed.
Lenin: And by the way.
Trotsky: (Moving down C.) It was late at night my wife and I had retired when assassins climbed over the garden wall and entered the house by way of the kitchen. Shouts and screaming, running feet in the hall, doors thrown open.
Lunacharsky: In other words.
Trotsky: My wife and I rolled under the bed. The door burst open with guns blazing. Rat–a–tat. Bing, bang. It was deafening. Then as quick as they'd come they were gone. We came out from under the bed unscathed. It was a miracle. The walls were pocked with bullet holes. We live in an age of devilment. (Not only that.) Thrones tumble, Empires break up, and new nations come to

life, regimes transformed in a twinkling. New orders introduce new men of power who go on inflicting ruthless experiments on the people. Freeze. Music in. Always the people. Blah, blah, blah. Millions imprisoned, Blah, blah. Exiled to Siberian gulags, Blah, blah, blah. Condemned to starvation, exposure, suicide, and systematic torture by sado–masochists. What matters is character, not intellect. The character of rulers has a powerful and lasting influence on the curse of events.

Kerensky: Of course you mean curse, I mean course?

Trotsky: What I mean is when you shoot the messenger and the one who sent him who's going to know?

Coachie: At any rate in 1917 Russia was bloated with pseudo intellectual fanatics and zealots driven by tremendous passion. I was with them. Now I'm with you. I'm with you. I'm with them. He's with us.

(All speak lines in brackets and carry pencils.)

Stalin: I harbor no illusions. (None.) I'm master of intrusion, (Not only that.) complicity and collusion. (In other words.) When I create you constipate. My thing is conspiracies. Real or imagined. I feel swell when I poison the well. Then the imperative periodic purge to cleanse the wayward urge. O, Lenin said this. Lenin said that. Lenin's dead, idiots! (Revolution in the West first. Industrial Europe must point the way.) Bread on the table points the way. I turned an abstract notion into reality. (In other words.) Mine was the iron fist of the pragmatist. With a toothpick and a steamroller, I paved the way for a forlorn country, yanked ignorant backward Russia kicking and screaming into the 20th century. (Not only that.) There is dogmatic Marxism and creative Marxism. I opted for the latter. I use people's vanity to my advantage. (In other words.) Kill or be killed. The secret to power is endurance, and sound biology. As to philosophic talk, bah! I'm a pragmatic predator. If it moves I eat it. Grr! They say Stalin is an evil genius who sees around corners. Bah! I decide what is there by setting it up in advance, and that's how I bend, and predict the future, ha, ha, you infantile bible believing bonehead lovers of falderal fairytales. I'm coming back for you, yes, you, and you. Even God can't stop me because there is no God. If God is the essence of man then it's buried with Lenin and Jesus Christ. Strike at night without pity;

use second and third parties (Then destroy 'em.) until the trail back is lost in tortuous paths (Converging, diverging.) with no way to prove (Who did what.) and truth is an owl hooting in the night. (Hoot! Hoot!) And by the way, Trotsky, you're a pencil freak intellectual Hebe, weaver of obscure scenarios that hang in the air like grapes on vines for birdbrains to peck at chirping epithets: Incisive! Revealing! Brilliant! Tfu! I gave you new life as a darling ex–patriot who ended up fucking that skinny Mexican Frieda. Did Diego know, or was that fat over–rated glutton too busy screwing your wife, and painting peasants? Writers are tall in the saddle, but short in the legs. High–minded eunuchs. I fooled everybody for 3 decades, except Hitler. Sent him food, supplies. I knew sooner or later he'd strike. Unfortunately, it was sooner. Next to Mamushka he's the only man who ever caught me with my pants down. O, we were devils, Hitler and I. But I was buying time like Lenin when you signed the Brest–Litovsk Treaty. I figured when the battle in Europe ends I'll knock off the exhausted winner. But that bastard Hitler couldn't be trusted.

Trotsky: Some people are in the gutter looking at the stars.

Stalin: You were looking in a mirror. How I'd love to kill you all again. (Ooooh!) Grr! (We believe, we believe!)

Trotsky: Tell you something about Lenin that completely eludes you. Lenin was corrective and educational never punitive or pernicious.

Stalin: Fuck him! "To smile and yet be a villain" is the sweetest food. Politics is the business of . . . Survival! (Flips him with a judo throw.) Lenin said you can't make a revolution with manicured fingernails.

Trotsky: (Rises; bows, dances around Stalin then punches him in the belly.) You fratricidal maniac. Shame on you. (They dance.)

Stalin: One day the gist of politics will hit you in the head like a bright bulb. The music of life changes, but never the steps. Right foot, left foot, round about. You're a Jew lost in Coyocan, Mexico. An Espan yid. I fucked you, Lev Sedov, your son, and the circumcised horse you rode in on. (Dancing off alone.) My dreams become other people's nightmares.

(Everyone whirls around. Trotsky partners with Lenin.)

Lenin: Always at the core of political life is the problem of power.
Trotsky: The old guard was driven by tremendous passion, heads reeling with no end of theories. (Wonderful!) Souls yearning for the good life, eager to re–direct the course of history, to say, life is not a pigpen. (Dances with Lenin.) We dropped the ball, Ilych. Forgive us.
Lenin: C'est la vie, mon ami. Few men change history, fewer die heroes. Most men exit broken and dispirited. (Broken and dispirited.)
Trotsky: We became bureaucratized, self–aggrandizing. I knew it was wrong, disgraceful, against all that's good and right in the heart. We took up the torch, stepped into a promising future, but when you died everything collapsed..
Lenin: Lev Davidovitch Bronstein. I like that name better Trotsky.
Trotsky: Between intention and implementation came biology with crushing finality. In the end I choked on a forgotten childhood lesson from the Realschule. After my classmates were caught booing a teacher they confessed and ratted me out for smoking in the boy's room. It was my first political test. Afterward, I divided the class into talebearers and the envious on one side, and the frank, courageous boys on the other, with the neutral vacillating mass in the middle. These three groups never disappeared even in later years. I met them again and again in life. Were it not for the vagaries of human destiny, the black humor attendant on mankind, and my disillusionment in the disparity between what men say and do; man's inability to grasp an idea; to trust, to rise above petty vindictiveness—well, Utopia might've been ours. The Greeks were right. The end is foreshadowed in the beginning.
Lenin: Truth and justice are not sufficient in themselves; there are no givens, no guarantees. Your ability to lead was never doubted, but you carried yourself with hauteur, which was offensive. You were a weathercock on issues and positions. I was always ready to bend on issues, but I would never waffle or compromise important principles. I was strictly dedicated to the cause to the exclusion of love, and petty sentimentality. I played the piano, you know, but rarely gave into it because music touches the soul, makes one soft when he must be hard. You tended to hear the music.

Trotsky: Certainly I gave myself to the revolution.
Lenin: But you lacked the ability to elicit devotion without ego.
Trotsky: I believed people who shared similar experiences who fought together, laughed and cried together, would in the end stick together.
Lenin: One would think so.
Trotsky: I thought the old shared experiences, battles won and lost, the camaraderie, that trust and intelligence, respect for disagreement, the pushing and shoving to achieve an unparalleled success would count for something.
Lenin: One would hope.
Trotsky: What happened was shameful. Comrades reduced to mindless animals begging for their lives. The party became what it most abhorred.
Lenin: Lev, dear, dear Lev. I kiss you with all my heart. It was given us to know the pain of the world, to say we don't need mandates or legislation to distinguish right from wrong, to express what is in the heart. In the time given us, how do we advance the sum total of all who have gone before us, who lived and died for truth and freedom?
Trotsky: Does death teach something that only death can teach?
Lenin: We shall soon see, comrade. O, your body feels warm. (Dance around.)
Kerensky: Lenin, confess. How did Lenin really die?
Lenin: In a mist riding a troika to utopia.
Stalin: (Down R.) If there is a heaven god will have to contend with me. All you polemic loving pencil pushing poets of politics, put this down: Your epitaphs will read: "Incidentally," "not only that", and "by the way". Mine will say, "King of Peppery Dishes!" Just give me a toothpick and a steamroller.
Tsar: It's all Dead Leaves Under the Bed.
Stalin: *I prefer the smell of comrades pissing their pants, begging for mercy. Where are you with your pencils? I stand with Caesar, Napoleon, and Peter the Great. Add this to your book. I am what is, not what might be. Hitler was egotistical and loud. I am your grandpa, the greatest fake on earth. On my watch nobody sleeps. I am darkest in the sunlight. I am what is, not what might be, a*

primitive, remorseless, and shameless. I act n' never ask why. To care destroys the fun. I leave it to pundit knuckleheads like you all. I am made possible by YAWL!—The star of the Greatest Show On Earth.

Lenin: Stop. Stop!

Trotsky: No. It's my pencil.

Lenin: Give it over.

Kerensky: En guard!

Trotsky: O, stand back, you sons–of bitches! Give me air! I need to breathe fresh air.

Inessa: (Cutting in.) May I have this dance? It wasn't the French people who sang the Marseilles. It was thugs, criminals, and murderers.

Lenin: It's the old egg homily. Attack them, Stalin. (Stalin: Grrr!)

Kerensky: What you started, the tyranny and carnage was insufferable.

Inessa: So are you.

Lenin: We shall pick up where Simon Bolivar was stopped by imperialism. In dying for freedom one of his countrymen said, *I die as one but shall return as millions.* That time is now! When you destroy a power base you open the door to anarchy and despotism. It's the duty of an all–Russian democracy, to say, we shall not repeat historic mistakes otherwise shame on you. Shame on this Congress if it gives one iota of credence to a man who unleashed a blood bath.

Svetlana: My father was guilty of many horrible acts, but much of the blame belongs to Beria. I was in the room when father died, but I couldn't bring myself to approach him. What could I say to the man who destroyed my life and so many others? It was difficult to accept that my father whom I loved in spite of everything was devoid of mercy, virtue, and justice. I believe Beria was behind a lot of what is attributed to my father. Beria was evil. He pandered father's fears, aroused the paranoia in him which led to the terrible things that went on. His inner circle headed by Beria was gathered around him. At one point father closed his eyes and had stopped breathing. Beria went near, listened, nodded, *he's dead*, started to smile, and puffed up his chest as he saw himself taking over. The others gave out a sigh of relief like a weight had been taken off their shoulders. Suddenly father opened his eyes and everyone was horror–stricken. Beria froze and reversed himself totally with obsequious epithets of joy kissing father's hand. Father stared at Beria with eyes of venom, a frightful stare of suspicion possibly that he'd been poisoned.

Mamushka: Suspicion always haunts the guilty mind.

Svetlana: Father's eyes turned yellowish. They spat with their glare on Beria and the others with pure hate; then he expired. Father died as he had lived: friendless, and bloated with rancorous enmity. If it is true that we are all willing victims, what is in Russia's character that inclines her to victimization? Perhaps we interpret Christianity's notion that salvation only comes through suffering.

Coachie: Russian holy water, Vodka with an Asiatic twist. If you ask me, what did you learn in life, comrade? I'd say, never turn your back, especially on the army and the secret police. They have guns and organization. Stalin feared them and one man in particular Marshall Michael N. Tukhachevsky. Trotsky appointed him to office. By age 27 he had distinguished himself as a military genius. General, in 1920 you marched into Poland, that victory equated you with Napoleon. Please tell us about the Galician fiasco.

Tukhachevsky: On May 8, 1920 Pilduski's Polish army had taken Kiev. The Bolshevik forces drove them back from Soviet soil. The question then became should we follow them into Poland? Radek, Rykov, and Trotsky said, no. Why stir up Polish nationalism? Lenin, Kamenev and Stalin said yes. *Go in. Drive them back.* This will then raise the possibility of a people's revolution. I was given the go–ahead. We drove them back to Warsaw. The Polish government trembled. Pilduski remarked later on that *it was a total disaster for us*. The Polish Prime Minister called for help from France and England. Meanwhile, a second Soviet army mostly cavalry had invaded southern Poland. Stalin was with them as a "political commander" or in plain military jargon Stalin was not a fighting general. General Budienny was poised to capture Lvov, or Lemberg, the capital of east Galacia. I had extended my line, but then the French had come to aid Pilduski forces. Moscow ordered General Budienny to forget Lvov and assist me. There was no reply for three days. Then, Budienny shifted directions drastically and

Pilduski was able to attack our flank, break our line, and force us to retreat. It was a disaster for us. Had Budienny followed orders the Polish counter attack would've failed. Trotsky and the others blamed Stalin for the fiasco. Stalin wanted the glory of capturing East Galicia. Pilduski admitted at the time his *position was hopeless. Our luck changed when General Budienny failed to attack our rear. Had he done so our case would've been completely lost.* Stalin's interference in the field of battle in military matters cost us great humiliation. He had *no field smarts under pressure*. He relied on chance and luck rather than strategy advised by superiors.

Coachie: My WW II experience testifies to Stalin's ineptness in military matters under pressure. Stalin was slow in reacting to the German invasion of the Ukraine. He ignored messages from his generals warning of a massive German build up on our border and daily maneuvers. Stalin dismissed it as exercises to mislead the West. When the Germans invaded Stalin was stunned, and couldn't be reached for eleven days. He never gave one order about what to do. Our lack of defense, and strategy was costly especially for Jews who were caught by surprise. The Germans overran the Ukraine in a total rout. We lost tens of thousands dead or captured, because Stalin our genius leader had done nothing, and refused to give us directives. It took the heart out us.

Svetlana: There's an old maxim: he that loses wealth, loses much; he that loses friends loses more; but he that loses his spirit, loses all. I feared for my soul, but I feared for Russia's even more. The people did not deserve the Romanovs or my father, whose insipid brutality developed into full blown delusions of persecution that were kept alive and fed by that vile Beria the most treacherous of all those father gathered around him. I believe that father built an organization, which grew out of control like a giant octopus that had him in its clutches and from which there was no escape. He had unleashed a monster with far reaching tentacles that could at any given moment consume even him. Everywhere he turned there was Beria, or someone equally despicable and capable of abominable acts. Father never talked openly about it, but I sensed toward the end that he had come to fear Beria most of all. I have no doubt that had father lived longer Molotov and Mikoyan would've fallen, and another purge would've ensued directed at the Jews.

Coachie: Life was never easy around your father. He was suspicious, inclined to paranoia to the very end.
Svetlana: As the end approached for father I watched his inner circle gathered around him in a mockery of grief especially the sinister Beria. I have to say while father did many bad things, I'm not excusing any of it, the record speaks for itself, but I believe Beria's hand was behind much of it more than father knew. Father was not blind to Beria but said nothing openly. He lived with silence and never expressed his feelings or attempted to confide in anyone. The burden of what he had done weighed heavily on him accounting for long periods of solitude when father sat smoking his pipe in silence. Father was not blind to Beria and kept him close, sensing at any moment the snake might turn on him, too. Before father died he glanced around and at Beria with suspicion that maybe Beria had poisoned him. Doubtless Lavrenty Pavlovich Beria had considered it. Assassination was never far from father's mind. He kept to a small circle of friends, rarely left the Kremlin where he lived behind armored doors. He rode to our country dacha in an armored car–
Coachie: Never by the same route twice. He'd tell his driver which route to take at the last minute and then switch roads.
Svetlana: It was difficult to explain to school friends why we lived behind a double wall of barbed wire fences with armed sentries and watchdogs.
Coachie: You're right. Your father's ears were always perked.
I recall one involving domestics. (Spot on:)
Stalin: Beria, what are you up to?
Beria: Come round the office and see for yourself–
Stalin: I am talking about the members of my domestic staff.
Beria: O, which ones?
Stalin: You know very well which ones. Understand me?
Beria: Frankly, no. I'm at a loss to understand. Tell me.
Stalin: You're a sly fox, but you don't fool me. No. You don't fool me. You think I'm blind, have grown too senile, and can't put two and two together
Beria: I have never doubted your mathematical skills.
Stalin: The numbers add up to a preponderance of Georgians on my domestic staff. How come? Lost your voice? My driver is Georgian.

Several guards are Georgian. My kitchen includes Georgians. I see Georgians everywhere.
Beria: Even in the mirror. We are Georgians. That is no state secret.
Stalin: You son–of–bitch.—
Beria: True. But, you yourself said it is a job requisite.
Stalin: Which does not extend to my house. There are Georgians under foot, oozing from cracks in the walls. Georgians in my dreams.
Beria: We're all Georgian: you, me, Kaganovich, even that new fat Krushchev is Georgian. We Georgians stick together. We can rely on each other.
Stalin: Think so? Eh? Those southern country bastards will cut your throat for a kopeck. I fired every Georgian on my staff. Did you know that? Yes. That puts an end to whatever you were planning. Ha. Beria, you have long ears.
Coachie: Listening devices everywhere. (Boo!) Beria was the only one who ever survived contradicting Stalin. He had a way of saying things and getting away with it. Towards the end your father grew more suspicious. Orders were carried out, but rarely discussed. Once in my carriage I overheard several reporters talking about Stalin's crimes. (Spot reporters. Coachie mumbles Dah; listens.)
Reporter 1: Khrushchev was no innocent himself.
Reporter 2: He was a man of his time.
Reporter 1: Brainwashed like the others to think Stalin was infallible. The collective farms never worked properly.
Coachie: Kolkhoz delo dobrovolynoe. Work on the farm or don't. It's up to you.
Reporter 1: The alternative is implied: Siberia. My grandfather worked on a kolkhoz, a collective farm, and lived in a barracka, an army barracks, a long wooden building with rooms, several families, and a shared kitchen. He remembered one woman, an alcoholic, who loved to dance. Every night she put an ash can lid on the floor, dance on it making such a racket that nobody could sleep. So grandfather calls the police. They take her away. Next day she's back smiling, says, what a beautiful police station. I

dance for the police all night. Wonderful! Please. Call them again. (Spot out.)

Coachie: Gradually, unfolded the real Stalin picture full of distorted truth. After the files were opened we saw that confessions made by the accused and those they incriminated were gotten by intimidation and torture. Many of the accused recanted and were ashamed to have incriminated innocent colleagues. It was Beria's doing under orders from Stalin. In time we realized a paranoid and a sadist ran the country. Nobody was beyond their reach. Strange as it sounds not everyone knew what was going on. The Central Committee plenary sessions were not convened. The Politburo met infrequently, and the periodic meetings established by Lenin were discontinued. So it was near impossible to know what was happening let alone take a position against unjust charges and proceedings or against errors and mis–conduct in leadership. The Political Bureau was left out of daily activities, which Stalin controlled.

Kerensky: What happened to Voroshilov?

Coachie: Kliment Yefremovitch was a dedicated old guard Bolshevik. Stalin barred him from the Politburo sessions. Voroshilov had to phone for permission to attend. Stalin actually suspected Voroshilov was an English agent, and had a listening device in his house. (Boo!) The record about Stalin must be corrected from all points of view historical, political, educational, and practical. Future generations should know what really happened to ensure that their lives would not be a house of cards on a foundation of sand. The Stalin years were a Byzantine madness; truth was a needle in a haystack. He used people to do his dirty work; then found ways to incriminate and dispose of them, obscuring witnesses and evidence that might lead back to the truth of what he'd done. I hesitate to say more, but we must be honest with each other. Your father planned to wipe out the entire old Political Bureau members while installing inexperienced people who knew nothing of the past, who would praise him for the wonderful job he'd been doing. A man would go see Stalin at his request, sit there, and not know at the end of the conversation whether he'd go home or to prison. If you dared to suggest a wiser approach to what he wanted, he'd thank you, and the next day you'd find yourself in Siberian Taiga. I woke up when Germany invaded Russia. Stalin took credit for winning the war as if he'd done it alone. He never visited the front, or looked at a map brought to him. He drew lines on a globe. He blamed his many blunders on others and took credit for the eventual successes like he'd foreseen everything. The real Russian victory belongs to its heroic people not to Stalin. (Spot on:)

Stalin: I signed an agreement with Ribbentrop, shook his hand, and agreed to partition Poland. Their attack was a total surprise.

Coachie: No, no. You had warnings from our military, foreign agents, German deserters, and Winston Churchill himself, but you ignored them and the outcome was a disaster. You practically handed success to the Germans when you purged the officer corpse of the best and most experienced officers.

Stalin: All subversives who colluded with the enemy,—

Coachie: Fabrication to distract from your failed programs.

Stalin: I had the traitors shot.

Coachie: And played into Hitler's hands. Don't try to sell us a wooden mug. The record must be set straight. During the war you displayed hysteria and nervousness, disrupting military operations causing us terrible losses. Terrible!

Stalin: You dare to say that to my face now.

Coachie: You never visited any sector of the front or any city before or after liberation. The truth is you are no Kuzma Kryuchkov. Now there's a Russian! Da! Kryuchkov, the well-known Cossack, initiated heroic feats against the Germans. He put on the dress of 7 people at the same time. Unlike you and most of our Party leaders, who were far from the guns and the blood and the dying, I had front line experience from WW I, which brought me in contact with the great suffering and courage of the Russian people. Forgive me, Svetka, but the lies end here. I began to see through his actions in the face of immanent annihilation. War heightens a man's survival instincts, and brings out his true character. In battle one learns fast who knows what, who has the courage of his convictions. War makes fools of leaders and heroes of plain people. America had Sergeant York and Audie Murphy. What we had was Stalin, a megalomaniac whose incompetence caused the death of over twenty million Soviet citizens, and the slaughter of countless Jews who had no warning of the Nazi invasion or its barbaric anti–Semitism. (To Stalin with mounting anger.) I was in the Ukraine when the Nazis invaded. Where were you? I was in the fight up to my eyeballs. Where were you? Those early disasters illuminated your wrong decisions under pressure, which glared at me with frightening reality. You did some good, dah, but the price in human suffering was enormous. In the thick of battle fighting with soldiers for our survival my gut led me to disagree with you for the first time. Suddenly, you were human, not superman. The incompetence of your cronies in key military positions in many battles cost us millions of casualties. Where were you, comrade? While battles raged, the slave–labor camps continued holding millions of men who might've helped us fight the Germans. Beria's police kept on arresting even more people. Unbelievable. In fact, your inability to act for the first eleven days following the invasion put us in grave danger. What was it? Eh? Cat got your tongue? What'd you have an anxiety breakdown, comrade genius? (To audience.) This same man who could toy with individual lives lost it in the heat of battle. I no longer saw him as the great genius and fearless leader. He blacked out for eleven days before he spoke to the people on the radio. Meanwhile, the Germans overwhelmed our forces, and took thousands of prisoners while instilling terror everywhere. There were desertions and defections resulting from incompetence and despair. I was in Stalingrad in 1941 when the Germans swept the Ukraine. I saw the red Army's heroic stand against enormous odds. (Picks up telephone.) Give me Moscow. Malenkov, where can we get rifles? (Spot on:)

Malenkov: Give up any thought of getting rifles. The rifles here have all been sent to Leningrad.

Coachie: What are we supposed to fight with?

Malenkov: I don't know? Pikes, swords, homemade weapons, anything.

Coachie: You are telling me to fight tanks with spears?

Malenkov: You'll have to do the best you can. You can make firebombs out of bottles of gasoline or kerosene and throw them at the tanks.

Coachie: (Hangs up.) Unbelievable! Then something unforgettable happened.

(Enter a general.) What is it?
General: The situation is hopeless.
Coachie: Keep your voice down, or you'll start a riot in the ranks.
General: Hopeless, I tell you. Hopeless.
Coachie: Then I was stunned. It happened so fast. The shock of that sudden final act so swift, unexpected. (General draws pistol, shoots himself; aides drag body off.) The blood, his brains everywhere. That was war. No two ways about it. Before my very eyes. (Picks up telephone.) The Kremlin. Stalin, Stalin! Kiev is being surrounded. We must pull back.
Stalin: No retreat.
Coachie: Hundreds of thousands of troops are strake.
Stalin: No retreat! No retreat! (Hangs up.)
Coachie: I sent for my commanding general. (HE enters.) General, the father of the Soviet people, the genius and master, refused to allow us to retreat.
General: My God. That is bad news.
Coachie: I'm countermanding his order. Ready the troops for withdrawal.
General: You want me to go against Stalin's orders? I can't. No, sir. I refuse.
Coachie: (Pulling out a pistol.) But Stalin is not here. I'm here. You will do what I say. Or by God I'll blow out your brains sending you straight to hell! (General salutes, goes out.) By the time he acted it was too late. We lost great numbers of troops and Kiev fell to the Germans. We had one success. In retreating from Kharkov, the second largest city in the Ukraine, I stayed at my command post to the very last minute so the Germans would suspect nothing. Before escaping by plane I had the building mined. I suspected the Germans would set up their command in my old post, a big mistake. Ha! The explosion killed many officers including the command general of the entire Kharkov campaign. In 1942 we tried to retake Kharkov. As we're advancing I could see something was wrong. (On telephone.) Stalin, we're entering a trap. We must retreat. Give the order to retreat. (Spot on:)
Stalin: You will continue.

Coachie: But it's clearly a trap. We'll lose a battalion needlessly. Give the order to pull back. I'm begging you. We'll re–group–
Stalin: (Overlapping.) No, no, no. Absolutely no retreat. (Rings off.)
Coachie: Okay, I thought. O–goddamn–kay! That's what you want that's what you'll get. God help us! I carried out his order but with vehemence.
General: (Entering.) Sir, we're entering a pincer trap. We must retreat immediately. Sir. Do you hear me? I urge you retreat before it's too late.
Coachie: I myself with my own hands, will blow out your brains. I'll shoot you to death like the lowest dog. I'll finish you off like the lowest scum of the earth! I order you, continue the offensive. (Exit general; looking out.) In ten days his army destroyed, the general phoned me saying it was *total disaster. I'm carrying out your threat to me myself.* (Two gunshots off.) He committed suicide and so did his aid. Our military leaders knew we were in trouble because of Stalin's wrong–headed tactics. Instead of flanking the enemy and attacking his back, Stalin insisted on frontal assaults, and our forces paid dearly for it. I brought in Zhukov, Russia's real hero general of the war. But from media accounts written on our Patriotic War you'd think it was Stalin. In the film The Fall of Berlin, we see Stalin alone, the master behind all our battle successes, giving out orders in a hall with empty chairs. Victory belongs to the heroics of our brave soldiers, and the entire Soviet nation. They won the victory. Women performed numerous acts of bravery on the front lines, in factories, on the kolkhoz. Our young people pitched in bravely in all areas and together, it was the people who turned the tide of war in our favor despite Stalin's interference. In 1943 when we re–entered Kiev it was a city of the dead. In the Ukraine 1946 there was a drought and poor harvest. People were starving, living in holes in the ground covered with anything they could find. I appealed to Stalin for help. He refused. The state took all the grain from the people causing famine and cannibalism. This *great leader,* father of the Soviet people, genius and master, had no feeling for the suffering and misery of others. After the war Stalin turned more capricious, irritable and brutal. He saw enemies everywhere. Beria took advantage of it as exemplified

by his bestial disposition toward the old guarder Kedrov, Golubiev, and his mother, Baturina. They spoke to the Central Committee about Beria's treachery, were shot without trial, and sentence was passed ex–post facto. These were Kedrov's last words on this earth:

Kedrov: I am calling to you for help from a gloomy cell of the Lefortosky prison. Let my cry of horror reach your ears, do not remain deaf, and take me under your protection. Please help remove the nightmare of interrogations and show that this is a mistake. I suffer innocently. Time will reveal the truth. I have never been an agent provocateur of the Tsaris Okhrana. I am no spy. I repeat I am no spy. I have never been a member of the anti–Soviet organization of which I am accused. I am guiltless of any crimes against the Party and government. I am an old, untainted Bolshevik who fought for 40 years in the Party ranks for the prosperity of our nation. I am 62 years old today and being threatened by investigative judges with severe cruel and degrading physical pressure. The judges are incapable of understanding that their handling of my case is illegal and impermissible. They justify their actions by describing me as a hardened enemy, and seek increased repressions. But let all in the Party know that I am innocent. There is nothing that can turn a loyal son of the Party into an enemy, even up to his last dying breath. But everything has its limits. My torture has reached the extreme. My health is broken, my strength and energy wan. The end is near. To die in a Soviet prison, branded a traitor to the Fatherland—nothing can be more monstrous to an honest man. Unsurpassed bitterness and pain grips my heart. No! No! This will not happen. This cannot be. I am certain that given an objective examination, without foul ranting, without anger and without fearful tortures, it would be easy to disprove the charges. I believe that truth and justice will triumph. I believe. I believe.

Coachie: The old communist was found innocent by a Military Collegium yet Beria had him shot. (Boo!) Comrade Ordzhonikidze tried to prevent Beria's shameful activities and told Stalin who did nothing and had his brother shot. It drove Ordzhonikidze to a state of anxiety and he shot himself.

Kerensky: It strains credulity that intelligent people could do such horrible things, could go so far astray as to engage in militant atheism, consider a regimented society without sentiment, the endless militarization of industry and the tireless search for a new enemy. You mentioned the kolkhoz. How many collectives were there?

Coachie: Several, not many.

Stalin: You don't want to work, don't work. Go to jail. And you, you stole a bag of flour? Twenty years in the gulag.

(Enter dancing Felix and Rasputin.)

Felix: (Gun in hand.) Grishka, you licentious, evil ragamuffin.

Rasputin: If evil is truth: guilty. (Felix shoots Rasputin; all freeze.) Is that it? Usually things come in threes. God's Trinity. Bing, bang, boom! Know what I mean? A fourth sound is out of place. There were three wise men. (Gunshot.) Three witches in Macbeth; three Graces in Greek. Hand me the oils. The blue bottle. (Falls.) In the name of the father, the son, and (Gunshot.) . . . Be that as it may . . . (Lights out, and up on:)

Trotsky: Sixteen years after Galicia Stalin's puppet prosecutor Vyshinsky accused General Tukhachevsky of participating in a "Military–Fascist organization" connected with Germany. In 1936 Tukhachevsky and seven generals were shot, an eighth one Garmerik shot himself. Stalin purged the entire leadership of the Red Army and thirty thousand officers died. The purge of the NKVD was also draconian. Yagoda, chief of the NKVD, secret police, was next because he knew too much. Yagoda, and thousands of his subordinates were purged. A five foot tall, unknown Nicholas Yezhov succeeded Yagoda. He introduced "Yezhovstchina", the biggest blood letting in Soviet history: Radek, Sokolnikov, and fifteen others died in 1937; Yagoda, Krestinsky, Bukharin, Radek, Rykov, and more in 1938; and the death of others without trial includes countless top–rank, second–rank, third and fourth–rank officials. Of the 27 Bolsheviks who drafted the 1936 Constitution for which Stalin took credit 15 were shot by 1938. Eleven Litvinov ambassadors were shot, Raskolnikov, who had a brilliant heroic Civil War record committed suicide. Entire faculties of universities vanished; foreigners who found asylum in Russia were executed;

thousands of journalists, novelists, poets, actors, playwrights, theatre managers, sculptors and painters were purged. With each prominent member of the party went dozens of his associates, friends, and relatives; cabinet members everywhere were purged, including their staffs numbering hundreds and even thousands. In time there was no one in the Soviet Union who did not have at least one relative or friend dead or in jail. The word in the street was: *He's not a Party member and he's not a Jew, so why has he been arrested?* Stalin liquidated Jews to bring on racist nationalism and instigate pogroms without him ordering them. In all purge cases and sudden disappearances, Stalin did not participate directly himself, but always behind the curtain one smelled smoke from his pipe. Another ploy was to dismiss magistrates who were obeying his orders including Yezhov—a technique meant to deflect blame from him, and turn eyes and anger toward subordinates. It promoted the age–old people's misconception that *it's not our fearless father but the swine below him who are to blame. If only our father knew the truth he'd fix them and change everything for the good.* Understand what I am saying? The fish always stinks from the head. 1939, after being on the job 3 years, Yezhov was purged. Yezhov's name is a curse. He's remembered as *the little man who was the biggest butcher in Russian history.* More than human beings died. You understand what I am saying? Something deeper than flesh and blood died. It was the Russian spirit, the hopes, dreams, and illusions—the flower of a new generation, brilliant, talented, on the threshold of a just society, a generation and a culture maimed, crippled, and murdered. Stalin was the Bolshevik Judas, the gravedigger of the Russian Revolution. (Hooting. Lights fade and up.)

Mamushka: V chuzhom glazu sonniku zametno, a v svoyam—brevna ne vidat. In another person's eye one can notice a mote but in his own cannot see even a log. Are your hands bloodied? And you? And you? (Each man drops his head.) And you. Are your hands bloodied?

Coachie: No. (Crosses self; thunder.) Yes! Up to here. (Touches shoulder.)

Mamushka: (To audience.) He that is without sin, let him cast the first stone. (Blackout; thunder, all cower with a look at Mamushka:)

End Part Two—Curtain Call Reprise
dancing with bows.

GLOSSARY

A bras ouverts—Open arms, cordially. abreaction—Removal of complex suppressed desire by talking it out, catharsis . . .

Aexander II—Assassinated 1881. Tsar Nicholas' grandfather

Alliluyeva, Nadezhda "Nadya" Sergeyevna, 20's,Stalin's wife; suicide 1931.

Archepelago—Chain of over a thousand islands, tree covered skerries; small islands stretching beyond Abot into Baltic Sea; any sea or broad sheet of water studded with small islands.

Armand, Inessa–Lenin's lover; bi–lingual; pianist; Party amanuensis.

Astrakhan—Russian apple; curled fur/skin of young karakul lambs; rough cloth imitating it.

Babushka—Endearment for mother.

Batyushka—Little father.

Bast—Strong woody fibers from phloem of plants like linden; used to make cordage.

Blanqui, Louis Auguste, 1805–1881;French; utopian socialist—initiated Paris Commune

Bible line (John 8:7.)

Bolshevik–Majoritarian; Divison of Communist Party after 1903; a communist.

Bourgeois–Middle class;bureaucracy; among radical socialists a person with private property.

Boyard—Boyar; Russian aristocrat next in rank below ruling princes; abolished by Peter the Great.

Brest–Litovsk Treaty–Between Russia and Germany 3.3.18; ends WWI for Russia.

Bukharin—Old Guard Bolshevik leader, d, 1938.

Bundists—Bund; began 1897; General Jewish Workers' League merged w/ Communist Party 1921.

Cadets—Constitutional Democrats—See Kadets.

Carpe diem—Sieze the day.

Carpe diem quam minmus credula postero—Enjoy today trust little to tomorrow.

Cheka—All–Russian Extraordinary Commission for Combating Counter–Revolution & Sabotage, 1917–22 state security service (See state agency)

Coachie or Coachman–a cabbie; story guide—narrator; formerly of high rank under Stalin.

Collectivization—Working together for good of state on state owned land.

Communism–Small political groups have power; goods held in common; classless society.

Da—Yes.

Don Bass or Donets Basin–South Russia area in Georgia.

Duma—Council, representative elected body w/ legislative power. Council of State or Russian parliament created by imperial order (ukase) in 1905. Discarded 1917 by Bolsheviks.

Defencist—Defending Russia; non–aggressive.

Expropriation–Lenin term for stealing money to support Bolshevik Party.

Faberge—Jewelers to the Tsar, noted for fancy jeweled eggs.

Figner, Vera—1852–1942; took part in assassination of Alexander II; spent 20 years in Schisselburg

Prison; see her memoirs about experience.

Galicia—In Poland.

Gorky, Maxim—playwrite–novelist died mysteriously 1936.

Gulag—Prison camps strung out in the archepelago.

Hall of Columns–Ornate hall of tsarists; nobleman's club, Moscow.

Haunts—A personal ghost; to recur in the mind.

Inessa Armand–Lenin's lover; bi–lingual; pianist;married to French husband with two children.

Iskra—The Spark newspaper founded by Paul Milyukov, an historian; 1st issue in Leipzig, 12.24.00; editorial board: Plehanov, Martov, Lenin, Zasulich; Plekhanov, Axelrod; Shipov

Izvestiya—Newspaper.

Jacobin—Fr. Rev; 1789–94; radical group instituted Reign of Terror; extreme radical espec. politics.

Kadets—(Cadets) Constitutional Democrats: Liberal, professors, middle of road. Semi revolutionary, non–socialists; wanted democratic parliament along British line; one of three parties dominating political scene, all but disappeared during the rural terror of War Communism.

Kaganovich, Lazar–B, Georgia; d, 1957 or 1967. Great organizer under Stalin; Jewish, cold heart.

Kalinnovka—Mud hut with thatched roof.

Kamuska–Gossip

Kaplan, Doris Fanya (Faena)—radical left social revolutionary;Lenin's would–be assassin 1918.

Kerensky, Alexander—Prime Minister–War Minister Temporary then Provisional Government 1917.

KGB—State Security, established 1954.

Kirov—1st Secretary of Communist Party, Leningrad province; second in command to Stalin; member of Politburo; assassinated 12.1934.

Kollantai—Bolshevik; old guard; became ambassador after revolution; free love advocate.

Kolkhoz—Collective farm.

Komsomol—Young communist league.

Konspiratsiya—Conspiracy

Kopeck—100 equals one ruble, i.e., about.60 American.

Kremlin—Kreml or fortress.

Kronstadt Uprising—Bulwark of original 1917 coup, insurgent sailors of Kronstadt 1921 demanded end to Bolshevik dictatorship and restitution of government by soviets as promised.

Krupskaya, Nadya—Lenin's wife.

Kulak—(tight fisted) richer peasant land owner; usurers of labor; preposterous, exploiting peasants.

Lev Sedov—Trotsky's son; killed 1938.

Lenin—b 1880; d, 1924 from either cerebral hemorrhage, poison, or venereal disease.

Limbo—State of being or place midway between extremes; forgotten past; hell's border; between heaven and hell, a place of imprisonment or confinement.

Long ears—Spies everywhere.

Luxemburg, Rosa—B 1871; Political agitator with Liebnecht and Jogiches, formed the Revolutionary

German Party: Spartacists. A martyr for Marx, Red Rosa or Rose le Rouge killed with Karl

Liebnecht 1.5.1919 in a failed Berlin uprising.

Mamushka—Mother.

Martov—Menshevik leader; split from Lenin around 1903 (?)

Matryoshka—Russian folk doll representing mother with several dolls within a doll.

Matushka–Little mother or good wife.

Menshevik–Minoritarian communist—Divison of Communist Party after 1903.

Moscow—Founded 1147 AD.

Muzhik—Peasant

MVD—Ministry of Internal Affairs; 1946.

Nadya Krupskaya–Lenin's wife.

Narod—The people; masses.

Narodniki—Populists; dark people; peasants.

Narodnaya volya—people's freedom, founded 1879

Nechego (Nee–chee–voh)—Nothing;empty pockets.

NEP—New Economic Plan.

Neue Zurcher Zeitung—News bulletin board by a lake in Zurich.

Nevsky Prospect—Huge public thoroughfare in Petersburg

Neva River—Running by Petersburg to the Baltic Sea

NKVD—People's Commissariat for Internal Affairs, preceded MVD. 1922–23, 1934–43.

Novaya Zhizn—New Life

Nyet—No.

Oblamov—Represents laziness, do nothing; character in literature who died from over eating.

Okhrana—Tsars Secret Service,1881–1917; about 10% of revolutionary groups were secret agents.

Orlov—Quality Russian horses bred and trained to pull the troika

OGPU—Political Police now the KGB. See State Agencies.

Paris Commune–Socialist group called the Commune took over part of Paris,3.1871, behind barricades; initiated what Engels called "first dictatorship of the proletariat."–or workers governing themselves. Ousted two months later by Republic. Protoype of liberated society with grass roots political system; admired by Lenin, Trotsky, and Mao Zedong.

Patronymic–Addition of ovich or evich to father's Christian name.

Petty Bourgeois: Lower middle–classs.

Pirogs—National pastry

Politburo—High level bureau of seven: Lenin, Zinoviev, Tomsky, Trotsky, Kamenev, Rykov, Stalin; then Kirov.

Populists–founded 1870's; terrorist acts against Tsaris regime.

Pravda—Russian newspaper means Truth.

Proletariat—wage earner; cut above peasant.

Provisional Government—followed the temporary government from May to October 1917.

Rasputin—dissolute monk; contributed to downfall of Romanovs.

Romanovs—Nicholas and Alexandra, assassinated 1918 Yatkaterinberg. Last of their line.

Ruble—Fifty cents to an American dollar.

Rykov—Bolshevik leader; d, 1938.

Revolution—There were three: March then October 1917; a third called the Civil War 1918–21.

So bachey—Dog cold . . . to sleep with your dog for warmth when it's very cold.

St Petersburg—Built by Peter The Great 16thc; Petrograd renamed St Petersburg in 1914 then

Leningrad; also Pete in slang.

St. Sophia—Monestary of the caves.

Shchi—Cabbage soup.

Simbirsk—A town north–east of Moscow birth place of Lenin and Kerensky.

Slava Bohu—Glory to God or Thank God.

Socialism—Collective or government ownership; democratic management of production & distribution of goods.

Soviets—Councils.

Spartacists—Revolutionary German Party named for Spartacus, slave liberator; Thracian gladiator opposed Romans.

Stalin—Man of Steel; B, 1879, d, 1953; Gori, Georgia, Ioseph Djugashvili early–on possible police informer; Party expropriator; unscrupulous, paranoid; misanthrope; alias Koba, So–so. Once many Stalin statues in Gori now only one. At times called hozyaen meaning boss or owner, head of family.

State Security Agencies—Secret police: Cheka or Extraordinary Commission to combat counter revolution, 1917–1922; changed to GPU or OGPU, Chief Political Administration or Political

Police, changed to NKVD or People's Commissariat of Internal Affairs; to MVD 1946 then KGB:

Committee of State Securit established 1954.

Starek—old man; boss; colleagues name for Lenin.

Subbotnik—A proletarian who works free on Saturday for the good of the state.

Svetlana—Daughter of Alliluyeva and Stalin

Troika—Russian carriage drawn by three horses; a group of three.

Trotsky—Leon Davidovitch Bronstein; Jewish, b, 1880 on farm in Ukraine; assassinated 1940 in Mexico. Lenin's heir apparent.

Tsar—Caesar; a king, emperor.

Tsarevitch—son of tsar of Russia; also grand duke; Cesarevitch.

Tfu! Spitting gesture to indicate feeling mostly negative.

Tumbrel—A cart used to transport prisoners; Fr Revolution 1789.

Uglich—Town north of Moscow

Urkas—Caste, highly developed underground culture; cutthroats; gamblers; mutilators, rapists; grotesque.

Utopia—A book by by Thomas More, 1516, describes an ideal commonwealth.

Varenyky–Raviolil filled with mushroom, potato, or cooked meat; with sour cream; Ukrainian.

Verst—A Russian measure of length, equal to 0.6629 mile, or 1,067 kilometers.

Volodya—or Vladimir sometimes Vovachka or Vova; endearment for Lenin.

Volga—Large river by Simbirsk, east to Moscow; connects Petersburg by Volga Baltic Waterway.

Voyzhid—Boss.

Vyshinski, Andrei—Stalin's puppet procurator.

War Communism—Militarization of labour to get industry back working. The Bolshevik defaulted on promise to abolish standing army; An illusion to transform semi–feudal into socialist economy.

White Guard—Anti–Bolshevik; from belye or white; coined by communists to discredit opponents; white was standard of Bourbons & 19th c French monarchists; gave impression opponents were monarchists.

Yagoda—KGB Chairman 1934–36 (.NKVD); shot after trial in 1938. Assisted in death of Kirov, Lev Sedov (Trotsky's son), Gorky . . . used "wrecking style" poison approach.

Yarosslavl—Town on the Volga headed east.

Yezhov—KGB Chairman 1936–38. (.NKVD).

Zemstvo—Organs of local government.

Zinoviev—Bolshvik; close associate of Lenin; died during purges mid 30's.

Z golovoy ne druzesh—You're not friends with your hat.

The Players: (Some double as other characters)

Act 1—Coachie, quasi repentant liar; Chiedze, party official; Marie Kollantai; Vladimir Bouch-Bruevich; Lenin; Nadya; Inessa; Kerensky; an Aide; Trotsky; Kransky; Stalin; Svetlana, his daughter; Bukharin; Lunacharasky; Zinoviev; Bogdanov; 2 Finn hunters; Galena; Uritsky; workers; soldiers; sailors.

Act 2—Kerensky, ex-War Ministry of the Provisional Government; his Aide; Lenin; Nadya; Inessa; Trotsky; Stalin; Coachie; Tsar; Tsarina or Sonny; Zinoviev; Lunacharsky; Bogdanov; Martov; Bukharin, Chief Party theoretician, later leader of the Right Opposition; Kirov, head of Petersburg government likely successor to Stalin; Doris "Fanny" Fanya; General Deniken; Party stooges.

Act 3—Trotsky; Lenin; Sverdlov, runs Party finances; Nadya; Inessa; Kollantai; Kransky, radical lawyer, assistant to Minister of Justice; Mamushka; Coachie; Kerensky; Zinoviev; Kamenev; Stalin; Uritsky; General Dzerzhinsky recently out of Lubianka; Lomov—pro Lenin; Sokolinikov-co-editor with Stalin of party journal; Varvara Yakovleva takes minutes; Rabble.

Act 4—Kerensky; Lenin; Nadya; Trotsky

Act 5—Lenin, Zinoviev; Shotman; 2 Finn hunters; soldiers; vigilantes.

Act 6—Lenin; Trotsky

Act 7—Coachie, also plays Nekita Sergeiyenich; Stalin; Svetlana Allelieyva, his daughter; Beria; his old retainer; Molotov; Voroshylov; Kaganovich; others; Mamushka looks on mostly ignored; Svetlana, daughter to Stalin. Not seen, Nadezhda "Nadya" Sergeyevna Alliluyeva, Stalin's late wife.

Epilogue—Bukharin; Kerensky; Kirov; Trotsky; Stalin; Lenin; Nadya; Inessa; Zinoviev; Gorky; Coachie; Tukhachevsky; Svetlana; Bogdanov; Lunacharsky; Rasputin; Felix Yusupov; Tsar; Tsarina; Mamushka watches from Cabbie's seat.